PUFFIN BOOKS

NICOLA MIMOSA

When her ballet teacher suggests that she should try for an audition for a place at the famous Kendra Hall, Nicola Bruce is over the moon. Her younger sister, Rose, is already at stage school and there's nothing her mother would like more than to have another daughter on the stage. But when she thinks about it, Nicola's not really sure she wants a career as a dancer and perhaps it would be better to stay on at school – her teachers think she should try for university and maybe become a doctor. She loves ballet but is she dedicated enough to sacrifice all those other things she enjoys, like biology, hockey and going to football matches? All her friends know that she's going to 'do' ballet – all, that is, except her boyfriend, Denny, and he has his own strong views on the matter.

It soon appears that everyone but Nicola knows what she should do. But it doesn't matter what they may expect of her, this decision will affect the rest of her life and she is determined to make it herself.

In this entertaining and lively sequel to *Hi There, Supermouse!* Jean Ure continues the story of the talented Bruce sisters.

Jean Ure was born in Caterham, Surrey, and her first book, *Dance for Two*, was published while she was still at school. She is married to an actor whom she met at drama school.

Nicola Mimosa
JEAN URE

PUFFIN BOOKS

Puffin Books, Penguin Books Ltd, Harmondsworth, Middlesex, England
Viking Penguin Inc., 40 West 23rd Street, New York, New York 10010, U.S.A.
Penguin Books Australia Ltd, Ringwood, Victoria, Australia
Penguin Books Canada Limited, 2801 John Street, Markham, Ontario, Canada L3R 1B4
Penguin Books (N.Z.) Ltd, 182–190 Wairau Road, Auckland 10, New Zealand

First published by Hutchinson Children's Books Ltd 1985
Published in Puffin Books 1986

Copyright © Jean Ure, 1985
Illustrations copyright © Martin White, 1985
All rights reserved

Printed and bound in Great Britain by
Cox & Wyman Ltd, Reading
Typeset in Garamond

1

'Look here!' Cheryl Walsh stabbed a finger on to the page of biology notes which she was copying from her rough book. She sounded aggrieved. 'What's this s'posed to be? *An*them?'

The question was greeted with silence, both her companions being preoccupied: the one practising ballet steps, using the back of the bench as a convenient barre, the other cramming her mouth with pieces of chocolate.

'I thought anthems were what you got in church. I didn't know *flowers* had them.' In red ball-point Cheryl drew a wobbly picture of something which might or might not have been a daffodil, or possibly a tulip. 'Anthem,' she wrote, and drew a big arrow. 'I thought anthems were things that you *sung*.'

More silence.

'*Well?*' said Cheryl. '*Aren't* they?'

'How should I know?' Sarah Mason broke off another piece of chocolate and laid it lovingly on her tongue. 'Ask her.' She jerked her head towards Nicola, still assiduously practising *battements tendus*. 'She's the expert.'

Since she was speaking with her mouth three quarters full of chocolate, this came out as 'Jeez theggzpirt.' Nicola, however, seemed to understand it. She paused, briefly, in her *battements*.

'Who said?'

'Zrijjson.'

'Miss Richardson? When?'

'Other day.' Sarah stashed her chocolate into a cheek pouch, there to let it linger and melt all by itself. 'When she was going on about me being lazy, and I said I was only lazy with things I didn't like and I didn't like biology and she said, well, that's up to you, but I won't have you distracting Nicola . . . I have High Hopes for Nicola Bruce. That's what she said.'

'Wonder what she meant?'

'Meant she had high hopes,' said Cheryl. Cheryl was an adept at stating the obvious. 'Thinks you'll go to university and study all about anthems.'

'An*thers*,' said Nicola. 'With an *r*.'

'Oh!' Cheryl peered more closely at her rough book. 'So it is . . . I knew anthems were what you got in church.'

'I nearly told her,' said Sarah. 'I nearly said, she's wasting her time 'cause you're going to do ballet.'

Nicola looked anxious.

'I hope you didn't?'

'I said I *nearly* did.'

'Why, anyway?' Cheryl, busy obliterating the word anthem beneath several layers of red ball-point, spoke without bothering to look up. 'Everyone knows you're going to do ballet.'

'No, they don't . . . *I* don't.'

'Your mother does.'

'She doesn't *know*,' said Nicola. 'Nobody actually *knows*.'

'She goes on as if she does.'

'Yes, well – ' Sometimes Mrs Bruce got a bit carried away. There was nothing she would like more than to have Nicola at ballet school. Then she would be able to

6

boast, 'My elder daughter, Nicola, who's training to be a dancer,' just as now she boasted, 'My younger daughter, Rose, who's training to be an actress.'

'Don't you want to?' said Sarah.

Nicola paused, one foot arched in its sensible school shoe (solid black lace-up with stout flat heel: Mrs Bruce wouldn't let her wear high heels or anything exciting).

'Don't know whether I'm good enough.'

'Course you are.' That was Cheryl again, stating what seemed to *her* to be the obvious. 'You're heaps better than Janice Martin.'

Anyone could be heaps better than Janice Martin. Being heaps better than Janice Martin didn't prove a thing, and even if it did – well, even if it did she still wasn't *certain*. Not absolutely one hundred per cent. Not enough to have people go round telling people, especially people like Miss Richardson, who had High Hopes. She looked over Cheryl's shoulder at the mess in her biology book.

'You don't spell photosynthesis like that.'

'So how d'you spell it?'

'With a ph – and a y in the middle. D'you want to copy mine?' She picked up her duffle bag and rooted through the contents: gym shoes, T-shirt, *Maths II, Africa Today*, breaktime apple which she hadn't yet eaten. 'Anyone want an apple?'

'No thanks,' said Cheryl.

'No thanks,' said Sarah.

Nicola pulled a face and put the apple away again. Denny would eat it; Denny ate most of the things she didn't want. Apples, yoghurt, horrible health-giving crunchy snacks from the Wholefood Shop, he wasn't fussy.

'Here you are.' She dropped her biology notebook on top of Cheryl's and turned, without too much hope, to

7

Sarah. 'Give us a bit of chocolate?'

'No,' said Sarah.

'Go on!'

'*No*.'

'Your mum'll go mad,' said Cheryl.

'My mum won't even know!'

'She will, she'll ask us.' Sarah, self-righteous, wrapped up the last few squares of chocolate. She did it very carefully, tucking in the edges and making a neat little parcel. 'She made us promise . . . don't let Nicola gorge herself.'

'I don't want to gorge myself! All I want is one teeny piece.'

'It'll show up,' said Cheryl. 'It's millions of calories, chocolate is. Millions and millions.'

Nicola sighed. There had once been a time, about three years ago, when she had been eleven, when she hadn't had to bother about calories. Mrs Bruce had even complained, then, that she was too thin and needed fattening up.

'Look at you,' she used to grumble, as if it were Nicola's fault. 'Skinny as a rake.'

Those had been the days of peanut butter sandwiches and strawberry milk shakes and as many helpings of chips as she could manage, in the hope that it would make her pretty and plump like her younger sister Rose. It never had, and it was Nicola's belief that it never would, for after all she was *still* skinny as a rake in spite of stealing everybody else's pudding on days when it was stodge and custard and sometimes, secretly, glutting herself on packets of popcorn and salted nuts. Nicola was so extremely skinny that a group of new and cheeky first years had even nicknamed her Spiderman, but now that she was going to be a ballet dancer and be as famous as Rose (who had always been going to be famous) Mrs

Bruce wasn't taking any chances: she was weighed once a week and measured every month. Not that anybody could do anything to stop her growing *up*wards – she was already taller than most of the girls in her class – but at least she could be stopped from growing *out*wards. It didn't matter so much if Rose grew outwards because with Rose it was just puppy fat and added to her charm, and in any case Rose was going in for musicals, not for ballet. As Mrs Bruce said, if you were going to be a ballet dancer then you had to be prepared to make sacrifices.

There were some things Nicola didn't mind sacrificing. She didn't mind sacrificing peanut butter, or liver sausage, or suet pudding, or even chips, but she did find it hard to have to sit by and watch as Sarah stuffed chocolate every break, and her stuck with nothing but a mouldy apple.

'You are a meany pig,' she said.

Sarah grinned. Like Rose, she was somewhat rounded, and on the short side: also like Rose, she was pretty. Rose was pretty in the way that kittens on chocolate boxes are pretty. She had big blue eyes and chestnut curls and dimply cheeks all pink and freckled. People said that Rose was adorable. No one would ever have said that Nicola was adorable – *or* that she was pretty. Usually, on account of her hair being dark and rather lank and because she didn't have Rose's pink-and-white complexion, they said that she was sallow, which was apparently not a desirable thing for a person to be. It didn't really bother her; not as much as it had when she was young, before Mrs French had discovered that she could dance.

'I'll give you one little square,' said Sarah. 'Just *one*.' She held out the packet. 'Here you are.'

Nicola hesitated.

'Well?' said Sarah. 'D'you want it or not?'

She wavered.

'You better hadn't,' said Cheryl. 'It'll put on at least a pound.'

'Oh! Disaster!' Sarah rocked melodramatically on the bench. 'Fatness and hugeness and things that go bump in the night!'

'Janice Martin goes bump in the night.'

'Janice Martin! Nicola couldn't ever get to look like Janice Martin.'

'She could, if she kept on eating chocolates.'

'She's not keeping *on* eating chocolates.'

'She is, she had some off you only last week, you'll make her go all pudgy and horrid so she'll be too big to dance, then instead of being able to say we were at school with Nicola Bruce all we'll be able to say is we were at school with her soppy sister.' Nicola's friends didn't think too much of Rose. 'Rose *Vitullo*.' Cheryl gave a simpering smile and stuck her fingers in her cheeks to make dimples. 'Honestly! I ask you.'

Sidetracked, Sarah said: 'Are *you* going to call yourself Vitullo?'

'No,' said Nicola. She said it very firmly.

Vitullo had been Rose's idea – it had been the name of a teacher they had once had, and Rose had taken a fancy to it. She had said that Bruce sounded too much like a dog. Now, at stage school, and whenever she did commercials or appeared in shows, she was Rosemarie (pronounced Mar*ee*) Vitullo.

'You mean you're going to stick to Bruce?'

'Why not?'

Sarah considered a while.

'I s'pose Nicola Bruce sounds OK.'

'Sounds better than Vitullo.' Cheryl finished copying Nicola's biology notes and handed the book back.

'Vitullo sounds Italian. She doesn't even *look* Italian. Why does she have to be such a stupid cow?'

'Oh, she's all right,' said Nicola. When all was said and done, Rose *was* her sister. One couldn't be too disloyal.

'All I hope', said Cheryl, 'is that *you* won't get like that when you go to ballet school.'

'Don't yet know if I'm going to ballet school.'

Nicola leaned with her back against the bench, tendrils of hair whipping into her face from the stiff March breeze which came flapping across from the Common. The field was full of the usual breaktime bustle, dotted all over with little knots of pupils wearing the red sweaters and blazers of St Mary's Streatham. Rose had never gone to St Mary's, she had moved straight from juniors to stage school – the Ida Johnson Academy of Dance & Drama, which was in London, in South Kensington, which meant that Rose had to take the mainline train up to Victoria every day and then go by Underground, which she enjoyed because it made her feel important. If Nicola ever went to full-time ballet school she supposed that she would also have to go up to London.

She frowned, and shifted her position slightly. Over by the sports pavilion a group of boys was kicking a football around. One of them was black, but she couldn't make out from this distance whether it was Denny or someone else. It might have been Denny. She screwed up her eyes, trying to see.

'You coming down the Body Centre Saturday morning?'

It wasn't Denny, it was a boy from 4G called Frank Woolgar. He looked a bit like Denny from a distance, but when she screwed her eyes up she could see that it was Frank because he wore his hair all long and

11

ringleted, whereas Denny's was cut short.

'*Are* you?'

A finger jabbed her in the ribs. She jumped, and looked round.

'Am I what?'

'Coming to the Body Centre Saturday morning.'

The Body Centre was a place where people went to do work-outs and improve their figures. It was also a place where you could, if you wanted, just sit around at little tables amongst the displays of leotards and leg warmers and drink milk shakes to the sound of the Top Twenty. Cheryl, Sarah and Nicola quite often spent an hour or two there before setting off on a shopping expedition.

'I can't this Saturday, I've got a class.'

'After class.'

'I can't after class.' After class she was meeting Denny and catching the bus to Selhurst Park to watch Crystal Palace at home to West Ham. 'I'm going to a football match.'

'What, with your dad?'

Nicola made a grunting sound, which might have meant either yes or no according to which way you interpreted it. Up until last season she *had* gone to football matches with Mr Bruce; but then she had discovered that Denny also supported Palace, and somehow or other she had started going with him, so that now Mr Bruce had to go on his own. It made her feel a bit mean, except that she and Denny liked to hold hands, which was something you couldn't very well do in front of a father. Not that Mr Bruce would have objected (Mrs Bruce might: she didn't care for boys) but he was a person who was very easily embarrassed. He would only keep looking the other way and pretending not to notice, and then that would embarrass her and Denny as well.

'Don't know what you see in football,' said Sarah.

(Nicola observed, with mixed feelings, that the chocolate had been put away and forgotten.) 'I can't think of anything more *boring*.'

'Once on television,' said Cheryl, 'in *Match of the Day*, someone's shorts fell down.'

Sarah looked at her, hopefully.

'Did you see anything?'

'No, they took the camera away.'

'That's what I mean,' said Sarah. 'It's so *boring*. Don't *you* think it's boring?'

She turned accusingly to Nicola, now doing a balancing act on the back of the bench, stretched horizontally across it with her legs in the air.

'Wouldn't go if I did, would I?'

'It's much more fun up the Body Centre,' said Cheryl. 'Why can't you come up there before?'

'Before class?'

'Before the football.'

''Cause I don't finish till 12.30. There wouldn't be time.'

'Thought you finished at eleven?'

'Not any more, it's been changed.'

It had been Mrs French's idea: if Nicola came from eleven till half past twelve instead of from ten till eleven, she could work with some of the more advanced pupils. The later time wasn't really as convenient, but obviously you didn't turn down an invitation to move into a more advanced class – *and* to have an extra thirty minutes. Nicola had three classes a week now, plus piano lessons every Tuesday with funny little dumpy Miss Caston, who had taught Rose. The rest of the time she had to spend catching up on her homework.

'Know what?' said Cheryl. 'I'm really glad that I'm not good at anything. I mean, dancing or anything. I mean, it's like being an invalid almost. Like that Miranda girl that played the cello and wasn't allowed to do games in

14

case she knocked her hands about, and Nicola not being able to eat properly in case she gets fat, and –'

'*I* eat properly.' Nicola swung herself deftly back to the ground. 'I eat properly, you eat junk.'

'I like junk.'

'Bad for you,' said Nicola. Rose ate junk, and Rose had spots, only you weren't allowed to say so. She anointed them every night with special spot stuff which was supposed to take them away. She got very touchy if you said anything.

From across the field came the sound of the bell summoning them back to the last classes of the day.

'Double bilge!' Sarah groaned. 'You'd think they did it on purpose.'

'Could be worse,' said Cheryl. 'Could be double maths.'

Nicola slung her duffle bag over her shoulder.

'Could be double *needle*work.' Needlework was one of the few classes which she really hated. She didn't mind maths, or French, or computer studies, and she positively enjoyed English and biology, but whenever they had needlework she ended up hot and cross. Mrs Hibbert had said to her, once, 'I'm surprised at you, Nicola! Surely you don't make all this fuss every time you have to darn a pair of pointe shoes?' She didn't, but only because it was a necessary evil and because Mrs Bruce wouldn't do it for her. She hadn't done it for Rose, she said, and she didn't see why she should do it for Nicola. If Nicola was going to be a dancer, then she must learn how to darn her own pointe shoes.

As they jostled through the swing doors into the main school building, Sarah suddenly leaned across Nicola and, pointedly addressing Cheryl in a loud stage whisper, said: 'Don't look now, but someone's coming. ...'

Nicola turned her head and saw Denny amongst

the crowd. Very solemnly, he closed one eye: equally solemnly Nicola closed one in return. It was their secret signal. The first wink meant, *Are we walking home together after school?* and the second wink signalled *Yes*.

Satisfied, Nicola peeled off towards the science wing for two periods of biology with Miss Richardson. Cheryl and Sarah peeled off with her.

'Ah! Love!' cried Sarah. 'What a wondrous thing!'

Cheryl swooned, and staggered into the wall.

' "My heart is like a watered shoot – " '

' "A singing bird", you idiot!' Nicola was too used to their taunts, by now, to be thrown into confusion. ' "My heart is like a singing bird –" '

'Well, you said it,' said Cheryl. She giggled. 'Not me!'

2

'Y'know Frank Woolgar?' said Denny.

'The one with the ringlets?'

'Yeah, the Rasta. Y'know what he said to me?'

'No?'

'He said I oughtn't to be going out with you.'

'What did he say that for?' Nicola was indignant. What business was it of Frank Woolgar's whom Denny went out with? And why shouldn't he go out with her, anyway?

'Says I'm betraying the cause,' said Denny.

'What *cause*?'

'Some cause he's in to ... black consciousness, or something. Says we all got to stick together.'

Nicola looked at him, rather anxiously.

'So what did you say?'

'What do you think I said?'

'Don't know –'

Denny grinned, and swung her hand.

'Told him to get stuffed, didn't I?'

Nicola relaxed. They wandered on across the Common, taking the path they usually took, which cut a direct line between Nicola's side of the Common and Denny's. After a bit: 'You know Miss Richardson?' said Nicola.

'One that does biology?'

'Mm. Know what *she* said?'

'What?'

'She said she'd got high hopes for me.'

There was a pause.

'What's that mean?'

'Dunno.' Nicola giggled, suddenly embarrassed by her own boasting. 'Probably not anything.'

'Probably means she wants you to take it for O levels.'

'Cheryl says it means she wants me to go to university.'

Seriously, Denny said: 'Would you want to?'

She wrinkled her nose, considering.

'Might do.' It all depended on whether or not she was good enough to get into ballet school. Mrs French had never yet suggested it. 'I s'pose I wouldn't mind.'

'What'd you study?'

'Biology,' said Nicola.

'What, you mean plants and things?'

'And animals.' And people. 'P'raps I'd do medicine and be a doctor.' She had thought of being a doctor, once; it was something she had almost forgotten about.

'What sort of doctor? In a hospital?'

'Mm . . . maybe. Maybe I'd go out and be one in India or somewhere.'

'Wonder if they have systems analysts in India?'

A systems analyst was what Denny was going to be: computer studies was his best subject. On the whole Nicola was more interested in people than machinery, it was only because Denny liked computers that she made an effort to keep up.

'Perhaps we could both go out to India.'

'Won't be for years yet,' said Nicola. It took ages to become a doctor. She calculated on the fingers of the hand which Denny wasn't holding: by the time she finished studying (if that was what she decided to do) she would be twenty-three. It was so far ahead as to be almost in another century. If she went to ballet school and became a dancer she would probably be famous by the time she was twenty-three. Maybe. 'Want an apple?' she said.

'Yeah, OK. Want half a cheese roll?' Denny stopped, dumped his briefcase on the ground, rummaged round a bit, and finally emerged triumphant with a small tinfoil packet. 'Here.'

Nicola hesitated.

'Go on!' Denny thrust it at her. 'Cheese and pickle, do you good.'

She took it reluctantly.

'I oughtn't really, I'll be having tea any minute.'

'Yeah ... one glass of fruit juice and a pot of yoghurt.' Denny knew all about Mrs Bruce's food régime; he didn't think much of it. He didn't think an awful lot of Nicola's dancing, either. He was one of the few people who didn't reckon that being a famous ballet dancer was such a big deal. 'You got to eat it, I saved it for you specially.'

'All right.'

Nicola undid the tinfoil and took out the half cheese roll: Denny munched on his apple. They walked for a while in silence.

'My mum,' said Denny, 'says you need fattening up.'

That was because Denny's mum was very large and plump. Mrs Bruce would have starved half to death before allowing herself to have hips the size of Mrs Waters. She had gone on a diet at the same time as she had made Nicola go on one and was now down to a girlish size twelve, which was what she had been before she had started having babies. Sometimes she put Nicola

19

to shame by going into changing rooms in shops that were really meant for teenagers and trying on short skirts and frilly dresses, just to show that she could still get into them. Rose didn't mind, she thought it was a great gas. She kept telling Mrs Bruce how her friends at stage school 'thought you were my sister'.

Oddly enough, Mrs Waters seemed every bit as happy as Mrs Bruce, in spite of not being a size twelve, or even a size fourteen, but probably about a size fifty, if sizes went that high. Every time Nicola called round there she tried feeding her gorgeous heavenly foods such as fried bread and fish and chips, which Nicola had to say no to (because however happy Mrs Waters might be there was no denying that she was hardly the right shape for *Swan Lake*).

'She reckons you're too thin,' said Denny.

'Not for a dancer, I'm not.'

'She says you'll fade right away if you're not careful.'

'That's all she knows . . . I'm tough as old boots. You just try me!'

Doubling both fists, Nicola flew round to the front of him and began pummelling at his chest, feinting and sidestepping as she had seen boxers do. Denny, with a jeer, dropped his briefcase.

'Go on, then, Muscles . . . hit me!'

After a long and bloody battle Nicola found herself spreadeagled on the ground with Denny sitting astride her, hands clamped over her wrists.

'Tough as old boots! You couldn't even strangle a chicken.'

'Wouldn't want to . . . that's *horrible*.'

'Someone's gotta do it,' said Denny, 'if you're gonna eat 'em.'

'Shut up!' She kicked at him, crossly. She didn't want to think about things like that, it gave her a bad feeling

in the pit of her stomach. How could she go on enjoying roast chicken every weekend if she kept thinking about people strangling them? 'Anyway, they're not strangled,' she said.

'No, they're hung up by their legs and have their throats cut.'

Just for a minute, Nicola felt sick.

'Shut *up*!' she said.

She kicked at him again; good-naturedly, Denny removed himself. Faintly, from far off across the Common, came the sounds of a clock striking the half hour.

'Heavens!'

In sudden panic, Nicola snatched up her duffle bag. Denny bent to re-tie a shoe lace which had come undone in the scuffle.

'What's the big rush?'

'I've got a class at half-past five!'

'So?'

'So I've got to get back and have tea.' She jittered impatiently, trying to hurry him. 'Come on!'

'All right, all right, I'm coming.' Grumbling, Denny picked up his briefcase. He had said before, and would no doubt say again, that if you asked him Nicola had a great many more ballet classes than were good for her. (What he really meant was that she had a great many more ballet classes than were good for *him*, because it interfered with other things he would have liked her to do, such as going to the youth club to play table tennis or going to the local park and kicking a football around.) 'You oughta stop doing all this ballet,' he said. 'It's very bourgeois.'

'*Bourgeois*!' She buffeted him with her duffle bag. 'Bet you don't even know what the word means!'

'I bet I do!'

'I bet you don't!'

'I bet I *do!*'

'So what's it mean?'

'Means it's dead ordinary and what all other girls want to do.'

'Like going into computers is dead ordinary and what all other *boys* want to do.'

'Not all.'

'Well, not all girls want to do ballet . . . Cheryl doesn't for a start. She says it's like being an invalid.'

'Yeah,' said Denny. 'I reckon she's just about right.'

Nicola widened her eyes, accusingly.

'I'm not like an invalid.'

'Yes, you are . . . *oh, Denny –*' he mimicked her, in a small, high voice not in the least like hers '*– watch what you're doing, you'll hurt me, you'll bring me out in bruises . . . oh, dear, now look what you've done, I won't be able to dance!*'

'Well, you *can't* dance, covered in bruises.'

'*No –*' still he mimicked her, going on tiptoe and doing a little twirl, ' *– and I bruise so EASILY!*'

Only when people are rough.' She pushed at him. 'Go away!'

'*Go away, go away*!' He flapped his hands, in imitation. 'Diddums nasty wough boy make nasty gweat bwuises on her?'

Nicola giggled, in spite of herself.

'You are a pig,' she said.

It was impossible to be cross with Denny. He and she might argue a lot, and quite often they disagreed, but they never became nasty or said things to hurt, as Rose and Nicola sometimes did.

It was twenty to five when she arrived home and Rose was already there, glutting herself on banana-and-sugar sandwiches and telling Mrs Bruce in great detail, between mouthfuls, all about a new singing teacher they had at Ida Johnson who was absolute heaven and was called Ricky and looked like a film star, and they all had to call him Ricky because that was the way he said he functioned best, and he had singled Rose out for special praise and said she had an 'exceptionally nice little soprano' and Susie Siegenberg was jealous as could be because he hadn't said a thing to her and she'd always fancied herself as a second Barbra Streisand, which just went to show.

Having told Mrs Bruce all about it, Rose then proceeded to go through it yet again for Nicola's benefit, even though Nicola had actually heard most of it while she was still outside in the hall (Rose having a peculiarly penetrating sort of voice which sliced through wooden doors and brick walls as if they were made of paper).

'. . . and his name's Ricky, and he said we were to call him Ricky because that was the way he functioned best, and –'

'I know,' said Nicola. 'I heard.'

She might as well have saved her breath: nothing could stop Rose once she was in full flood. Not even Mrs Bruce interrupted. She gave Nicola her tea – which wasn't yoghurt but bran crackers and honey, with a piece of seed cake to follow – and waited patiently until they had come back again to Susie Siegenberg and her terrible raging jealousy.

'She's absolutely jealous as a *cat*.'

'Why a cat?' said Nicola, but nobody took any notice of her.

'It's silly to be jealous,' said Mrs Bruce. 'Jealousy never got anybody anywhere, least of all in the theatrical profession. She's going to meet a whole lot of people with better voices than hers, so she'd just better make up her mind to it. And why were *you* so late, my girl?'

24

Nicola, taken by surprise, choked on her bran cracker. It was Rose who answered.

'She was over the Common with that coloured boy.'

'Coloured boy?' said Mrs Bruce. 'Which coloured boy?'

'One she goes round with. I saw you,' said Rose. 'I was on top of the bus and you were fighting.'

Nicola swallowed her bran cracker.

'We weren't fighting, and you oughtn't to talk about people being coloured, it's rude.'

'It's not rude.'

'It is rude, they don't like it.'

Rose reached out for a piece of seed cake. (She always smeared hers with strawberry jam.)

'So what I am supposed to say? *Black*?'

'If that's what people are.'

'Well, he isn't, is he?' Rose sat back, contentedly, lips smeared with jam. She obviously felt that she had scored a point. 'He's cocoa coloured.'

'Who is?' said Mrs Bruce. 'Who are you talking about?'

'S'pose you'd like me to say that *cocoa coloured* boy?'

Nicola felt her knees begin to prickle. It was a bad sign: it meant that she was allowing Rose to rile her. Determinedly she helped herself to another bran cracker.

'You could always try using his *name*.'

'Don't know his name.'

That was a lie; of course Rose knew Denny's name. They had all of them been at juniors together. She was just pretending not to know in order to be awkward.

'Can't call someone by their name if you don't know it, can you?'

'In that case I don't know why you referred to him at all.'

'Because I was explaining why you were late ...
because I saw you with him over the Common.'

'So why couldn't you just say you saw me with a
boy?'

'You don't say you saw someone with *a* boy when you
know *which* boy.'

'Well, if you know *which* boy –'

'I wish,' said Mrs Bruce, 'that one of you would kindly
answer my question!'

They stopped and looked at her.

'You know perfectly well I don't like you going over
the Common. Who is this boy?'

Nicola wondered, for one tempting moment, what
Rose would do if she were to say John Smith or Elvis
McNaughton (which was the name of a boy Rose had
once sat next to in juniors.)

'Well?' said Mrs Bruce. 'I'm waiting.'

'It's Denny,' said Nicola.

'And who's Denny?'

'Boy in my class.'

'Boy who lives in those horrible council flats over on
the Wentworth Road Estate,' said Rose.

Trust Rose to know that. Nicola slipped a square of
bran cracker off her plate and slid a hand surreptitiously
beneath the table.

'You're too young to have boy friends,' said Mrs
Bruce.

Under the table, a mouth opened and the bran cracker
was gone.

'You can't afford the time, you've got your ballet
lessons to think of, not to mention all your school work
– and just stop feeding that dog! His manners are quite
bad enough as it is.'

'I'm not,' said Nicola. (Under the table, Ben thumped
his tail: he was a dog who never could keep secrets.)

'You are, I saw you! If there's any more of it, he'll be locked away.'

Nicola pulled a face: they had heard that before. Ben was always going to be 'locked away', to teach either him or Nicola a lesson. Once, actually carrying out her threat, Mrs Bruce had shut him in the garden shed, but Nicola had crept out there and sat with him and after only a few minutes Mr Bruce had appeared and accidentally-on-purpose left the door open and let him escape, because Mr Bruce was what his wife called a soft touch and didn't like having to teach people lessons. It was always Mrs Bruce who handed out the punishments, like the stopping of spending money and the going to bed without any television. (Not that Nicola minded about the television, especially if one of Rose's commercials were on. *Especially* the one for Dreamy Liquid, the liquid cleanser that pours like cream, and Rose at her most nauseating, simpering and pouting and being Mummy's little girl.)

'Eat up your tea,' said Mrs Bruce. 'You've already made yourself late enough, hanging around on the Common . . . I've told you before, I don't like you going over that place. Anything could happen.'

'Not with Denny.'

Rose, at this, gave a knowing cackle. Nicola looked at her haughtily.

'What's that s'posed to be in aid of?'

'Not with *Denny* . . . *I* saw you, rolling on the ground!'

'Don't tell tales,' said Mrs Bruce; and then, to Nicola: 'What were you up to?'

'Wasn't up to anything. I fell over.'

'Ha ha,' said Rose. 'A likely tale.'

There were times, even now, when she could cheerfully have *bashed* Rose.

'In future,' said Mrs Bruce, 'you come straight home,

27

do you understand?'

'Can't if I've got something on at school, can I?'

'Don't be cheeky! You know quite well what I mean. I don't want any loitering, especially over that Common. Do I make myself clear?'

'S'pose so.'

'Well! Do I or don't I?'

'*Yes.*' Nicola snatched irritably at a piece of loathsome seed cake. She wasn't giving up walking home with Denny just because Mrs Bruce had a hate thing against boys. She wasn't stopping going over the Common, either. If they tried walking down the High Street holding hands some busybody would be bound to see them and tell Mrs Bruce. They would just have to find a new route, somewhere out of sight of people who sat on the tops of buses and then came home and *blabbed*.

'If you wanted,' said Rose, 'you could bring him to my birthday party.'

'Bring who?'

She would make Rose say his name if it killed her. Rose licked a finger and began dabbing it round her plate.

'Denny Waters. If you don't think he'd feel out of it.'

'Well, he would,' said Mrs Bruce, 'obviously. All your friends are theatrical.'

'I know,' said Rose, 'isn't it *awful*? I just can't seem to get on with ordinary people.'

'Ordinary people lead different lives, that's why.'

There was a silence. Dab dab dab, went Rose with her wet finger, blotting up the crumbs. Under the table, Ben laid his big shaggy dog head lovingly on Nicola's knee.

'If *I'm* going to come to the party,' said Nicola, 'then I'll need someone like Denny to keep me company . . . I

28

wouldn't want to be the only *ordinary person* there.'

'You're not ordinary,' said Rose. 'At least, not as much as you used to be before you started ballet.'

'Yes, and talking of ballet –' Mrs Bruce tapped a finger to her watch.

'All right, I'm going.' Cunningly, as she pushed back her chair, Nicola slipped a piece of seed cake into the ever-open mouth beneath the table. 'I still don't see why theatricals are any different from anyone else. They're only doing a job, same as everybody has to. They're only earning a *living*.'

'That's what you think,' said Rose.

'That's what I *know*.'

'You don't know anything!' Rose's voice had become shrill, as it tended to in moments of stress. 'Acting isn't a job, acting's a *vocation*.'

'Crud,' said Nicola.

'Crud yourself!'

'Crud with knobs on!'

'Crud with – '

'BE QUIET THE PAIR OF YOU!' Mrs Bruce banged on the table with the handle of a knife. 'Rose, get on with your tea! Nicola, you go upstairs and get yourself ready – and STOP FEEDING THAT DOG!'

3

There are two basic types of dancer, those who are loose-limbed and supple, with high-arched feet and graceful arms, and those who are shorter and stockier, good at all the quick sharp movements known as *allegro*. Rose had always been one of the short stocky ones, Nicola one of the loose-limbed and supple. Being supple had definite advantages when it came to adagio work – Rose had never been any use at adage, her *attitudes* and *arabesques* had no style at all and her *ports de bras* were simply unspeakable – but was not so helpful for allegro. Rose could flash about the stage like a tadpole in a jar, her footwork as precise and exquisite as the tiniest stitches of embroidery: Nicola just occasionally had difficulty with footwork, and although she could jump quite high and always landed beautifully there wasn't very much that she could do while she was actually in the air. (Rose, according to Rose, had once done an *entrechat dix*. Nicola was never absolutely certain whether or not she believed this – she thought, on the whole that she did not – but it was a fact that Rose could be neat and nimble without even, apparently, having to try.)

Mrs French had always paid particular attention to Nicola's allegro. Just recently she had been paying even more attention than usual – 'It's purely a question of concentration' – which was why Nicola now had an extra, private class every Wednesday evening. One Wednesday, at the end of a specially gruelling session, Mrs French said, 'Go and get changed, then come down and have a coffee. There's something I want to talk to you about.' Nicola's heart instantly plummeted. Was she going to be told that her allegro was still so unspeakably awful (like Rose's *ports de bras*) that there simply wasn't any point her continuing to take classes? She honestly hadn't thought it was a awful as all that. She'd been trying really hard, and even if she *had* messed up on one perfectly simple *pas de bourrée* –

'By the way,' said Mrs French, 'that was good just now, wasn't it? Didn't you feel the difference?' Nicola gaped. 'Heaps better! You see, it's purely a question of concentration . . . off you go now, while I organize a coffee.'

Relieved, Nicola scuttled off to the tiny changing room, which once upon a time had been a Victorian pantry and still had a row of bells above the doorway saying BEDROOM 1, BEDROOM 2, BEDROOM 3. She wondered, as she peeled off her tights, what it was that Mrs French wanted to talk to her about. Last time she had invited Nicola to stay behind and have a coffee it had been to tell her that she was expecting a baby 'some time in June', but that Nicola wasn't to worry, she still intended to go on teaching. Nicola had been glad about that, because nice though babies were she wouldn't like the thought of Mrs French giving up classes just to settle down and be a housewife and wash nappies all day. She would hate the prospect of having to go and have classes with someone else – she couldn't bear to go to Madam Paula, as Rose had done. Madam Paula was a hag, who plastered herself in layers of make-up and wore jangly bracelets and dingle-dangle earrings and dyed her hair an unnatural-looking black. Mrs French was blonde and slim and beautiful, or at least she had been until her stomach started to swell up. There was no denying that having babies did make one rather an odd shape; all big and bulbous and sort of sticking out in front like a ledge. You wouldn't think a tiny thing like a baby would take up so much room. She hoped Mrs French wasn't going to say that she'd suddenly discovered she was expecting twins and would have to settle down to wash nappies after all; not now that Nicola's allegro really *was* heaps better. She was sure it wouldn't go on being better if she had to dance for anyone except Mrs French.

Suddenly anxious, she pulled on her clothes and hurried upstairs to the big living room, with its floor-to-ceiling windows and old-fashioned fireplace. Mr French was in the living room, sorting through a pile of glossy magazines. Mr French was a photographer, who took photographs of people who had just got married, or whose babies had just won beautiful-baby competitions. He also took photographs of well-known actors and actresses and gorgeous bony models. Last year, before she had become friends with Denny, Nicola had gone through a phase of thinking she might be in love with Mr French, which had been exciting but also rather embarrassing, because it meant she kept blushing every time she saw him and couldn't speak for lockjaw, so that on the whole she was glad she had grown out of it and could now manage to be in the same room without betraying herself. It had been very inconvenient always breaking out like a beetroot.

'Hallo!' Mr French looked up and smiled as Nicola came in. (This time last year she would have been solid beetroot from top to toe.) 'You're looking worried. What's the problem?'

'Mrs French wants to talk to me.'

'Really? Well, I don't suppose it's anything terrible . . . might even be something nice!'

Yes, like *I've suddenly discovered I'm going to have twins.*

32

That probably would be something nice, for Mrs French. Mrs French would probably be quite excited about it. Perhaps Rose had a point when she said she was never going to get married, and that even if she did she was never going to get pregnant. Getting pregnant ruined things. Mrs French didn't look anywhere near as beautiful as she had before – and it was all Mr French's fault.

Nicola glared at him, feeling for a moment quite cross. In return he waggled an eyebrow and pulled a funny face.

'I'll photograph you one day, if you're a good girl and don't frown at me. You've got a good face for photographing; lots of interesting angles. Did you know that?'

She shook here head, suddenly shy again. She had always thought Rose was the one with the good face.

'Give it a year or two, you might even make a model. Have your picture on the front of the glossies. Like this –' He held up a magazine for her to see. On the front was a girl with long hair and not many clothes. Nicola regarded it doubtfully. She didn't think she would like to be a model if it meant being photographed three quarters naked. 'Or this one –' Mr French held up another. The girl on this one was fully clothed, but even so Nicola remained doubtful. It seemed rather a silly thing to do, just standing around being photographed.

'What are you up to?' The door was pushed open and Mrs French came in carrying a tray and three coffee mugs. 'I hope you're not trying to talk Nicola into becoming a model?'

'Why not? She'd make a very good one, she's exactly the right build, got exactly the right type of bone structure.'

'That's as may be. I happen to have other plans for her.'

Oh? Nicola spun round, wonderingly. This was the

first she'd heard of Mrs French having any plans.

'How would you like to try for a place at Kendra Hall?'

'*Me?*'

'Yes, you!' Mrs French laughed, as she set down her tray. 'Who else would I be talking about?'

'But –'

'But what?'

'Would I be good enough?' Kendra Hall was where Mrs French had gone. You had to be really something to get in there.

'If I didn't think you were good enough,' said Mrs French, 'I wouldn't be suggesting it, would I? Mind, there are a lot of people applying and only a very few places, so don't get your hopes up too high. I happen to think you stand an excellent chance, but being good enough from a dancing point of view is only the start of the battle. There are all sorts of other factors to be taken into account. Height, weight, general health . . . they'll want to check your feet, check your back, make sure you're not going to grow too tall, make sure you'll be strong enough –'

'Far simpler,' said Mr French, 'to be a model.'

'Nicola doesn't want to be a model!'

'How do you know? Ever asked her?'

'I don't have to ask her. She's too good a dancer and she's got too much sense.'

'Is that so?'

Mr French turned, and cocked an eyebrow in Nicola's direction. Fortunately, since Nicola didn't know what to say, Mrs French said it for her.

'Of course it is! No fourteen-year-old devotes herself to hours of hard slog every week just for the fun of it. It's not like stamp collecting, or joining the Girl Guides. You have to be pretty devoted, you know, to undergo the rigours of a ballet training.'

'Pretty insane, if you ask me.' Mr French winked at Nicola as he removed his coffee from the tray. 'I'm afraid it's all a bit too high-powered for us lesser mortals. I shall make myself scarce and leave the lunatic fringe to get on with it.'

'Right.' Mrs French spoke briskly. She patted the sofa. 'Come and sit down, and let's talk. How much do you know about Kendra Hall?'

By the time she left, Nicola knew a great deal. She knew that it was up in London, and that she would have to travel there every day by either bus or train and then the Underground. She knew that the Hall itself was an ancient manor house, that it had its own grounds where the pupils could play tennis or netball (but not hockey, for fear of broken limbs) and that it had its own theatre where shows were put on every term.

'A beautiful little place – used to be stables, in the old days. You'll love it, I know you will.'

Mrs French seemed every bit as excited as Nicola. She gave her a form, which had to be signed by one of her parents ('Perhaps you could ask them tonight? The sooner we get it off, the better') and a copy of the prospectus showing a picture of the Hall, with photographs of various classes and the names of all the staff and the subjects which they took. On the last page was a long list of pupils who had become famous, or at least well known. Under F it said, *Pamela French, former member of the Royal Ballet, now teaching*.

'Just think,' said Mrs French, 'your name might be there one day . . .'

Nicola thought about it all the way home, which actually wasn't long as home was only a few hundred yards down the road and most of that she covered in an exuberant series of *grands jetés*, leaping from crack to

crack in the pavement. The family, including Ben, were all in the front room, snug with the heating turned up high. Rose and Mrs Bruce were sitting in front of the television watching their favourite soap opera, all about life backstage at a famous London theatre. Every few seconds, as they watched, Rose would shriek or groan or roll her eyes, just to demonstrate that she *knew* what life was like backstage and it wasn't like that: Mrs Bruce would say consolingly that that was because the series was meant for 'ordinary people', and not for real professionals such as herself.

'Ordinary people like to think they know what goes on, even if it is a bit exaggerated.'

Mr Bruce, who was as ordinary as could be and didn't care tuppence, was sitting in the corner smoking his pipe and reading one of his gardening books. Ben was the only one to look up as Nicola came in. He grinned, and thumped her a welcome from the hearth.

'That was a long class,' said Mrs Bruce.

'It wasn't all class,' said Nicola. 'We were talking. I've got a form for you to sign . . . it's for me to go to Kendra Hall.'

'Kendra Hall?' Rose bounced round in her chair. 'You'll never get into Kendra Hall!'

Some of Nicola's excitement fell away from her.

'How do you know?'

'They're ever so snooty, they never take anyone.'

'They've go to take *some*one.'

'A girl at Ida Johnson tried three times and they didn't take her.'

'So what?'

'So she was really *good*,' said Rose.

'Obviously not good enough.' Mrs Bruce leaned forward and switched the television off. Rose let out a wail.

'Don't do that! I want to know what happens!'

'Well, you'll just have to wait till Monday, we can't talk with that thing blaring away. Where's this form I have to sign?'

'Here.' Nicola pulled it out of the back pocket of her jeans, together with the prospectus. 'It's this bit where it says *consent of parent or guardian* . . . we've already filled in all the rest, all you have to do is just sign it and then we can send it off.'

'And then what happens?' That was Mr Bruce, from within his clouds of pipe smoke.

'Then they send her a date for an audition.'

'And what happens if she's accepted?'

'Well, then they offer her a place.'

'She won't be,' said Rose. 'People never are. Not unless they're progenies.'

'Prodigies,' said Mr Bruce. 'What sort of place are we talking about? Full-time, or –'

'Full-time, yes.'

'You mean she'd have to leave St Mary's?'

'Well, obviously!' Mrs Bruce held out a hand. 'Lend me your pen.'

'Before you sign anything,' said Mr Bruce, 'you don't think perhaps we ought to discuss it?'

'Discuss what? What is there to discuss?'

Mr Bruce turned, and knocked out his pipe. (Mrs Bruce tutted crossly as some of the ash fell to the floor.)

'Isn't Nicola a bit young to be taking this sort of decision?'

'At fourteen? On the contrary, I should say she's rather old.'

'Fourteen's practically middle-aged,' said Rose.

'Middle-aged!' Mr Bruce laughed. 'Hark at the child!'

Rose didn't like being laughed at – or being called a

38

child. She tossed her hair back, angrily.

'Well, it is! Most people start when they're only five.'

'Exactly,' said Mrs Bruce. She reached for her handbag and began rooting through it in search of a pen of her own. 'If Nicola doesn't decide now, she might just as well forget about it.'

Mr Bruce frowned.

'Are you seriously telling me that by the time she's old enough to leave school it would be too late?'

'As far as ballet is concerned, yes.'

'So at the age of fourteen she's expected to make a decision which could affect the whole of the rest of her life?'

'It's a big chance,' said Mrs Bruce. 'She can't afford not to take it. It's a question of now or never.'

Mr Bruce shook his head. Rose, who had sneaked forward and switched the television back on, but with the volume turned down to escape attention, settled herself contentedly in front of it.

'Course, you don't actually *have* to go when you're still young . . . Susie Siegenberg's sister didn't go till she was almost seventeen.'

Nicola looked at Rose resentfully. Whose side was she on? (And who was Susie Siegenberg's sister when she was at home?)

'It's only people that are really dedicated that go as soon as they can.'

'You can't be really dedicated at fourteen,' said Mr Bruce. 'You're not old enough to know your own mind.'

'I was!' shrilled Rose. 'I was dedicated at only *nine*!'

'In any case –' Mrs Bruce finally ran a pen to earth and put her bag back on the table '– the younger you start, the more chance you stand. If we'd discovered earlier that Nicola could dance, I'd have sent her to the Royal Ballet School when she was eleven. But of course we didn't realize.'

'It was her own fault,' said Rose. 'Always going round being all butch and playing football . . . she didn't even *like* ballet. She kept saying it was soppy.'

Nicola, kneeling on the hearth rug doing Ben's ear out for him with her little finger, wondered if Rose really were as dim as she sometimes seemed to be, or whether it was simply that she was so bound up in herself and her own affairs that she never bothered to stop and think about other people and what made them do some of the things that they did. Had she not worked out even yet that when Nicola had said ballet was soppy and gone off to kick footballs, it had all been in self-defence and to solace her wounded pride? Because when people called you things like Spiderman, and Nicola Long Legs, and everyone said how gawky you were, how clumsy and awkward and unco-ordinated, what could you do but act tough and pretend not to care? Of course, Rose probably wouldn't understand because no one had ever said that Rose was clumsy or awkward. Rose had always been the dainty, charming one; there hadn't been any need for her to go and kick footballs and make out she was butch.

'What I want to know', said Mr Bruce, 'is what happens if she gets to this place and then after a couple of years she changes her mind? Suppose she suddenly decides she doesn't want to be a dancer after all? Then what do we do?'

Mrs Bruce looked at him in exasperation.

'You didn't say that about Rose!'

'Oh, well, Rose.' Mr Bruce hunched a shoulder, as if disclaiming all responsibility for Rose. 'You'd already made the decision.'

'Anyway,' said Rose, 'it's different for me. I couldn't do anything else.'

Nicola knew that when Rose said she couldn't do anything else she didn't mean she wasn't capable of doing anything else but that nothing on earth was ever going to make her. Rose was very single-minded. She told everybody that life wouldn't be worth living if she couldn't get up on stage and act ... 'I'd rather *die*.' Nicola wouldn't rather die, she thought that was a bit silly and melodramatic, which probably just went to show that she wasn't as dedicated as Rose. In fact, now she came to think about it she quite obviously wasn't. Rose would never dream of going to football matches, or playing hockey, or reading books that weren't about the theatre: she would have considered it a waste of time. Perhaps she was right, and it was 'different' for her.

All the same, it wasn't every day you were given the opportunity to audition for a place like Kendra Hall, and, dedication or not, Mrs French seemed to think she stood a chance. She couldn't understand why her father was making all these objections; usually he just went along with whatever Mrs Bruce said, especially when it was to do with education.

'She got it!' said Rose. She sat back on her heels, in disgust, in front of the television. 'Cora got the part! That's *stupid*. She'd never have got it in real life. In real life they'd just have told her to go away and do something else ... that's really *stupid*.'

'Turn that box off,' said Mrs Bruce.

'But I want to watch! It's *Magic Master*.'

'I don't care what it is, turn it off.'

'But I *said* I'd watch! One of the boys at Ida Johnson – '

'You heard what your mother said,' said Mr Bruce. 'Turn it off.'

Sulking, Rose did so. Nicola removed her finger from Ben's ear and held it out for him to inspect.

'The thing that bothers me,' said Mr Bruce, 'is that Nicola's a bright girl –'

'So is Rose!'

'Not in the same way. Nicola's academic. Look at that report she had last term . . . came top of nearly everything.'

Nicola was impressed: she hadn't known her father ever bothered to read her school reports.

'She only came top of English and biology,' said Mrs Bruce.

'Well, then, near the top. Almost everyone, as I recall, said she was a good worker or showed great promise.'

'She obviously shows great promise as a dancer, or Mrs French wouldn't be putting her in for the audition.'

'They put in hundreds of people,' said Rose.

'Then that's all the more reason, if she gets through, that she goes ahead and does it. You couldn't ask for much more confirmation than that . . . accepted by a school like Kendra Hall.'

'It's not the Royal Ballet School,' said Rose.

'It's not far off it! Don't you start getting jealous, my girl, just because you were no great shakes as a ballet dancer.'

Wonders would never cease! Mrs Bruce actually *admitting* that Rose was no great shakes at something? (It was quite true, looking back on it: Rose's arabesques had been decidedly wobbly, and her pirouettes had been all over the place. She had never had what Mrs French called 'line'.)

'I could've done ballet,' said Rose. 'The only reason I didn't was 'cos Mrs French said I had too many other talents and it would be a shame to waste them.'

Rose was always so *modest*, thought Nicola. She put her face close to Ben's so that they could touch tongues. (Rose said that that was a disgusting thing to do. She said it was a wonder Nicola didn't contract some vile and ghastly disease.)

'The point I'm trying to make,' said Mr Bruce, repacking his pipe, 'is that Nicola also has other talents but that hers lie in a different direction. She ought at least to be given the chance to take some O levels before being pushed into anything.'

'We take O levels!' shrieked Rose.

'So they do at Kendra Hall,' said Mrs Bruce. 'It says here – ' she read from the prospectus, ' "*Pupils enter for general education examinations at the ordinary level in the following subjects . . . arithmetic, French, English language, English literature, history, geography, human biology, art and music.*" I should have thought that would be enough to keep anyone happy.'

'And what about the other thing she was talking of doing? Physics, chemistry, whatever it was?'

'You don't need physics and chemistry,' said Mrs Bruce, 'to be a dancer.' She removed the top from her pen and spread out the application form. 'Nicola, stop slobbering over that dog and go and get an envelope . . . we'll get it sent off straight away.'

4

'Nicola Tolstoy –'

'Nicola *Mark*ova –'

'Nicola Markova!' Cheryl slammed down her desk lid, triumphantly. 'That sounds good! Why can't you be Nicola Markova?'

Nicola, perched on the window sill of 3A's classroom pretending to study the view, didn't bother pointing out that there had already been a dancer called Markova. She left that sort of thing to Janice Martin, who had done ballet ever since she was eight years old and reckoned she was the world's leading authority. Sure enough, her voice came clanging across the room: 'She can't be Markova, there's already been one!'

Cheryl, unmoved, tore open a packet of bacon-flavoured crisps and crammed a handful into her mouth.

'I've never heard of her.'

'Never heard of Alicia *Mark*ova?'

'Never heard of *Nicola* Markova.'

'I didn't *say* Nicola Markova.'

'Anyway,' said Nicola, 'I'm not having a stage name.'

Cheryl turned, and looked at her reproachfully.

'Dancers always have stage names!'

'Not always.'

'They do if they're English.'

'Like Margot Fonteyn.' That was Janice Martin again, showing off. She was going to tell them all how Margot Fonteyn had started life as Peggy Hookham. '*She* started off as Peggy Hookham.'

'Anyone would change if they were called Peggy Hookham,' said Nicola. Across the field came a group of boys. She craned to see if Denny was among them, but he wasn't.

'It's got to be something Russian,' said Sarah.

'Barishnykov – '

'Ul*an*ova – '

Nicola turned back to the window. She hoped Denny arrived before classes started, she wanted to tell him about the audition. She had told Sarah at the school gates, and already the news had spread round half the third year (the female half: the male half remained steadfastly unimpressed) but it was Denny she really wanted to tell.

'Nicola Shostakovich – '

'Nicola Tchai*kovs*ky.'

'You ought to have a name ready,' said Sarah. 'Then you can be known by it right from the start.'

Nicola frowned, and wrapped one leg round the other. They all seemed to be assuming that simply because she'd been put in for an audition she'd as good as been offered a place. It was going to make it all the more difficult when she failed to get in. (*If* she failed to get in. Rose didn't know everything. Mrs French thought she stood a chance.)

From inside the stationery cupboard, where she was self-importantly counting paper clips in her rôle as stationery monitor, came Linda Baker's voice, somewhat muffled. It seemed to say, 'Doan cown chinz.' There was a pause.

'Don't *what*?' said Sarah.

'Doan cown chinz,' said Linda. *Crash*. That was the box of paper clips gone. (Serve her right, thought Nicola. Anyone who could bother counting paper clips every day needed her head examining.) 'Mikuzun*anj*ler – ' scrabble, scrabble on hands and knees ' – three gole *mells*.'

'Really?' said Sarah. She sounded rather bored. They had been hearing about Linda Baker's cousin Angela and her three gold medals ever since junior school. 'Just because *she* didn't get in doesn't mean Nicola won't.'

As as for counting chickens – was *that* Denny? – it was the last thing she was likely to do. Nobody could count chickens with Rose around.

'Talent runs in families,' said Cheryl. (No, it wasn't Denny. She bet the lazy pig and gone and overslept.) 'Like that Miranda girl that played the cello and had a sister that did it as well.'

Someone said: 'What's that got to do with anything?'

'Well, it's like Nicola doing ballet and having a sister that's at stage school . . . it's talent running in families.'

From inside the cupboard came what sounded like a snort. Janice Martin, who everybody knew was jealous because she'd been at Madam Paula's the same as Rose, the only difference being that Rose had got somewhere and she hadn't, flicked back her single, solitary, mouse-coloured pigtail and said: 'Stage school! Anyone can get into a *stage* school. You don't need talent for that sort of thing.'

Nicola turned, from her watching position at the window.

'What sort of thing?'

'Well – ' Janice waved a hand. '*Dreamy Liquid* . . . I ask you!'

'That's commercials,' said Nicola. 'She only does

46

them for the money. Anyone would.'

'*I* wouldn't,' said Janice.

Nicola sniffed.

'You wouldn't get the opportunity.' Rose might be absolutely foul, but she wasn't having some great useless flabby creature like Janice Martin run her down. At least Rose was good at what she did. When she'd played Amy in *The March Girls*, at a real West End theatre, *The Stage* had said that she was 'pert, pretty, and altogether irresistible'. Nobody could say that of Janice Martin.

'Thing is – ' Cheryl stuffed her last few bacon-flavoured crisps into her mouth and scrunched up the empty packet – 'even when she does Dreamy Liquid she's got *some*thing. I don't know what it is, and whatever it is –' the scrunched-up crisp packet flew through the air, landing yards away from its objective, which was the waste paper basket ' – whatever it is it's absolutely *yukkish*, but then it's *supposed* to be yukkish. Children in adverts are *always* yukkish. It's what people like. It's just that Rose manages to do it more yukkishly than anybody else.'

'That's *right*.' Sarah nodded. 'Like when she played that *really* yukkish part in the West End.'

'Amy.'

Somebody said, 'Vomit, vomit!' and clutched at her stomach. Several people obligingly made vomiting noises. They could laugh, thought Nicola, but they'd all gone along to see the show and been happy enough to be taken back-stage afterwards and visit Rose in her dressing room. Some of them had even asked her to sign autograph books – for their little sisters, so they *said*. Linda Baker, who didn't have a little sister, had actually, unblushingly, claimed that it was for her mother.

'Hey!' Sarah suddenly poked at her. 'There's your boy friend!'

Nicola, taken unaware, spun round. (She always

intended to remain very calm and offhand and not respond when people referred to Denny as her boy friend, because only let them think for a moment that things might be serious and they tended to get silly and start on the stupid jokes and ho-ho-look-who's-coming routine.)

'Who are you talking to?' she said, but she had left it too late.

Sarah grinned and wagged a finger.

'*We* know who you went to the football match with . . . *we* saw you walking down the High Street together.'

Honestly! Nicola shook her head crossly. It seemed there was no privacy to be had anywhere in this town. If it weren't Rose spying from the tops of buses it was Cheryl and Sarah goggling through the windows of the Body Shop.

Denny was ambling across the field as if he had all the time in the world instead of a mere sixty seconds before the bell rang for Assembly.

'Did you want him?' said Sarah. Before Nicola could stop her she had flung open the window and was leaning out, shouting. 'Oy! You! Lover Boy . . . your sweetheart's waiting!'

Denny stopped and looked up. As he did so, Miss Camfield, who was their class teacher, passed beneath the window. She, also, stopped and looked up.

'Sarah Mason,' she said, 'what are you doing leaning out of that window screaming like a fishwife?'

Sarah withdrew, giggling. Under cover of the general rush to get to the window (everyone being anxious not to miss out on the fun) Nicola made good her escape. She bumped into Denny as he was half way up the stairs. He jerked his head in the direction of 3A's classroom.

'What's all that about?'

'It's only Sarah, don't worry. Nobody takes any notice of her. Listen, I've – '

'What's she going on like that for?'

'*I* don't know, I s'pose she thinks it's funny. It's pathetic really. People are so childish. Why are you late? I wanted to talk to you, I've got something to – '

'Nicola Bruce and Dennis Waters!' Miss Camfield had caught up with them. 'What are you doing, idling in the corridor? Didn't you hear the assembly bell? Stop chitter-chattering and get to your classroom.'

'Listen,' hissed Nicola, 'I'm going to have an *audition*.'

'Audition for what?'

'Ballet school.'

'What ballet school?'

'Kendra Hall.'

'What's that?'

'Did you hear what I said?' said Miss Camfield.

Nicola put her hand over her mouth: 'Tell you later.'

'Nicola Bruce! How long have you been at this school? Long enough to know the rules – and you, young man! Just get a move on! Whatever it is, it will have to wait. It can't be as important as all that.'

Probably, to Miss Camfield, an audition for ballet school wouldn't seem very important because Miss Camfield took them for sports and as far as she was concerned ballet was just a nuisance. It meant that every so often, when Nicola had a dancing exam coming up and couldn't afford to run the risk of pulled ligaments or strained muscles, she would have to drop out of the hockey XI, or the rounders team, or the special gymnastics group, and a replacement would have to be found. Miss Camfield accepted the necessity, but it didn't stop her grumbling.

'You girls and your wretched ballet dancing! Is it really worth it?'

She knew that neither Denny nor Miss Camfield considered that it was, but she had thought that Denny, being Denny, might be just a *little* bit excited for her. Instead, when finally she managed to get him on his own (which wasn't easy, in a school of eight hundred pupils: spies lurked round every corner) all he said, rather grumpily, was: 'What's all this about ballet school?'

'I've got an audition! At least, I've applied for one.'

'What for?'

'What d'you mean, what for?'

'What d'you want an audition for? You're already at a ballet school.'

'Not a proper one. Mrs French only takes a few pupils, Kendra Hall's full time ... I'd be having classes every day!'

'*Ballet* classes?' Denny sounded incredulous. 'Every *day*?'

She nodded, earnestly.

'You have to, if you're going to be a dancer.'

'Thought you were going to be a doctor and go to India?'

'That was only if I didn't do ballet. I still might, if I don't get in – which probably I won't. Not many people do. I don't really expect I stand much chance. Mrs French thinks I might, but – ' she gave a little laugh, just to show she wasn't boasting ' – I don't expect I will.'

'So what're you bothering to try for?'

'Well, just in *case*.'

Denny said 'Humph!' and picked up a stone. Nicola watched as he flung it, with some force, towards the bicycle sheds. She wondered what his problem was – anyone would think he didn't *want* her to try for ballet school. Maybe he was just in a mood about something. She racked her brains, trying to think what.

'You know that maths test?' she said. 'One we had this morning?'

'What about it?'

'I only got four out of ten.'

'So?'

'What did *you* get?'

'Ten.' Denny said it aggressively, as if she should have known better than to ask. Denny always did get ten, or at the very least nine. It would be a bad day if he got anything less.

Well, he hadn't got anything less, so that wasn't it.

There was a silence. Denny flung another stone; Nicola thrust her hands into her blazer pockets.

'There's your sister over there.'

Denny grunted, obviously not impressed.

'Saw her this morning.'

'It's a pity she never did ballet.' Nicola studied her, as she strolled with a friend across the playing field. Denny's sister was sixteen, and in Class 5. She was tall and athletic, with long, strong legs that were made for running – or for turning pirouettes or doing *grands battements*. 'I bet she'd have been good at it.'

'She's gonna be a nurse,' said Denny. 'What's she want to do ballet for?'

'Might have decided to become a dancer, instead.'

'Why?'

'Why not? In any case – ' Nicola pounced, before the moment could be lost ' – what's she want to be a nurse for? Why not a doctor?'

'*I* dunno.' Denny hunched a shoulder. 'Never asked her.'

'Girls always choose to be nurses. It's like girls being air hostesses, and secretaries, and *house*wives. You don't get men being any of those things – well, sometimes you do, but not very often.'

'So what?' said Denny.

'So it's rôle-playing,' said Nicola. Miss Richardson,

this term, had been talking a lot about rôle-playing. It was something she felt strongly about; so did Nicola. 'We've got to break away from all that sort of thing.'

Denny jeered: 'Women's lib. crap!'

Nicola felt her face grow hot, and prickles break out all along her spine.

'You hadn't better let Miss Richardson hear you say that!'

'Miss Richardson's a dyke,' said Denny.

Nicola clenched her fists.

'She's nothing of the kind, you sexist pig! And even if she was, what would it matter?'

Denny at least had the grace to look ashamed. He scuffed a toe in the moth-eaten grass which bordered the playing field.

'Anyway,' he said, 'you need brains to be a doctor.'

'Your sister's got brains!' Denny's sister had passed nine O levels, which was more than Denny was likely to pass unless he started working a bit harder at some of those subjects he claimed to despise, such as English and French. 'I bet she could get to university as easy as pie.'

'Bet you could, too,' said Denny.

'Yes, but it's different for me.' (Horrors! Echoes of Rose . . . .) 'I mean, I don't actually *know* that I could get to university, whereas if I *did* get into Kendra Hall . . . not that I expect I will, but if I *did* – '

'You could always turn it down,' said Denny.

She stared at him, shocked.

'I couldn't do that!'

'Why not?'

'Well, because . . . because I *couldn't*. People *don't*. It'd be like turning down the Nobel Prize, almost.'

Denny looked at her. She coloured slightly.

'It's only a ballet school,' said Denny.

'Yes, I know.'

'It's not like working for peace, or discovering a cure for cancer.'

'I *know*. I didn't mean that. All I meant was that lots of people try to get in and hardly anybody does, so that if you're one of the ones that does – well, it means you've got to be *some* good. That's why I think your sister ought to be a doctor, because she'd be good at it and because there aren't many women doctors and *I* think there ought to be more of them. Specially *black* women doctors. I bet there probably aren't any black women doctors in this country at all, hardly. That's another reason why she ought to do it. It's important for people to set examples' (that was what Miss Richardson had said) 'especially when people are oppressed, like women and –'

'My sister's not oppressed,' said Denny. 'She's a pain.'

'*Women* are oppressed, and *black* people are oppressed, and – '

'You know something?' said Denny. 'You're starting to sound like Frank Woolgar.'

Nicola tossed her head.

'I'd rather sound like Frank Woolgar than a chauvinist pig! At least Frank Woolgar *thinks*.'

'Thinks a load of rubbish.'

'It's not rubbish! Not all of it. Some of it is – ' like saying Denny oughtn't to go out with her; that was rubbish '– but not everything. I mean, fighting for a cause . . . people *ought* to fight for causes.'

'Well, I'm not.' Denny stated it fiercely. 'I'm not fighting anything for no one, and specially not for people that go round trying to lay down the law about what other people ought to do.' Nicola wasn't sure whether he was referring to her or to Frank Woolgar; to both of

them, perhaps. 'I'm not fighting no wars, and I'm not fighting no causes, and I'm not – '

She never discovered what else Denny wasn't going to fight, because at that point there was an interruption: the bushes behind them suddenly erupted and Sarah and Cheryl burst through.

Sarah said 'Oops! My apologies,' and giggled.

Cheryl said '*So* sorry. Didn't know you were here,' and also giggled. Denny glowered at them, as if they were something nasty that had crawled out of a dunghill.

'What d'you want?'

'Oh! Pardon me, I'm sure.' Cheryl clapped her hand to her mouth, stifling another burst of giggles. 'We didn't realize anything *important* was going on.'

'Had we done so,' said Sarah, 'we should never have materialized.'

'Certainly *not*.'

'It would absolutely never have occurred to us.'

'Abso*lute*ly.'

'If we'd known you were having a *summit* meeting –'

'Why don't you just belt up?' said Denny.

He stalked off, across the field. Sarah stared after him.

'What's his problem?'

'He doesn't like people spying on him,' said Nicola.

'*Spying?*'

'*Us?*'

'Yes, you,' said Nicola. 'You're just about the dead end, you two.'

5

On Saturday, Rose had her party. It didn't start until six
o'clock in the evening, which seemed an odd sort of
time, but Rose wouldn't have it in the afternoon. She
said that afternoon parties were all right for ordinary
people, who went to ordinary schools, but 'in the profession' people didn't come properly alive until after
midnight.

'Well, you're certainly not having a party that goes on
till midnight,' had said Mrs Bruce.

'*After* midnight. One oughtn't really to start until
nine o'clock.'

'Rubbish! You'll start at six and finish at eight-thirty,
that's plenty late enough.'

'Well, so long as we can have a buffet supper,' said
Rose.

'What do you mean, a buffet supper? What's the matter with a sit-down tea?'

Everything, it seemed, was the matter with a sit-down
tea: a sit-down tea was for children, and ordinary people.
It had been all very well when Rose was small, but not
now that she was *thirteen*. She screeched with horror
when Mrs Bruce suggested jellies and trifles and angel
cakes with pink icing.

'Not for a buffet supper!'

'So what sort of things do you want?'

Mrs Bruce had seemed baffled. As a rule, she and Rose

understood each other very well (far better than she and Nicola, who scarcely ever saw eye to eye at all) but on this occasion Rose had obviously jumped one step ahead; Mrs Bruce had not yet had a chance to catch up. To her a birthday party was only a birthday party if there were balloons and crackers and funny hats – and, of course, jellies and trifles and cakes with pink icing. Rose scoffed at the idea. What she wanted was a party like 'the ones they have in the studios'. Last year Rose had been in a television production of *Children of the New Forest*, and at the end of filming there had been a party for all the cast and the crew at which champagne had been served, and lobster patties, and sausages on sticks: that was the sort of thing she wanted.

Mrs Bruce, for once, had stood firm. Lobster was out of the question, and so was champagne. She didn't care if Rose *had* drunk it at the television party. She didn't care if all Rose's little friends at Ida Johnson were in the habit of guzzling it down like tap water, they were not going to do any guzzling in Number 10 Fenning Road.

'I'm not having a horde of drunken thirteen-year-olds staggering about the place.'

Rose had grumbled and said that everyone would think they were mean. She had said she wasn't having fizzy lemonade because fizzy lemonade was too childish for words, and why couldn't she pay for the lobster patties out of her own money, which she had earned?

'It's cruel eating lobsters,' said Nicola. 'They put them in boiling water while they're still alive.'

'You shut up!' shrilled Rose. 'It's no crueller than eating anything else!'

'Yes, it is.'

'No, it isn't!'

'Yes, it *is*.'

'No, it isn't, what about cows? They kill *them* while they're still alive, don't they?'

Nicola fell silent. She wondered why it was that whenever she argued with Rose she always seemed to come off worst. Mrs Bruce came off somewhat better by the simple expedient of exercising parental authority: she said that Rose was not frittering away her earnings on lobster patties and that was that.

At this Rose had gone into the most tremendous sulk and threatened to tell everyone that the party had been cancelled, 'And what's more I'll tell them it's because of you! Because you're too mean and stingy to let me spend my own money!'

'You can tell them what you like,' said Mrs Bruce.

'I will! I'll tell them you've suddenly gone barmy and been taken into a mental home!'

'I probably will go barmy and be taken into a mental home,' said Mrs Bruce, 'if there's much more of this.'

For a day or two it had looked as though there weren't going to be any birthday party. Nicola told Denny that it had probably been called off and Denny said good, that meant they could go to the cinema instead and see *Wars of the Thirty-Ninth Galaxy*. They had almost definitely arranged it when Rose and Mrs Bruce reached a compromise: there was still not going to be any champagne, but they could have some bottles of sparkling apple juice, chilled in the fridge, and if Rose wanted to pretend it was champagne then that was up to her. As for lobster patties, said Mrs Bruce, she could make them with crab meat and no one would know the difference.

'You can always tell them it's lobster if that's what you want.'

'So long as *she* doesn't go and say anything.' Rose looked venomously at Nicola, who tossed her head.

'Why should I bother spoiling your childish games?'

By six o'clock on Saturday the table in the front room was all laid out with crab patties and sausages on sticks. There were bowls of crisps and salted peanuts, there were dishes of stuffed olives and platefuls of water biscuits spread with garlic butter, and cubes of yellow cheese with bits of gherkin or salami skewered on to them. Rose was happy and said those were exactly the kinds of things that her friends liked to eat. Rose's friends must have very peculiar tastes, that was all Nicola could say. She had sampled little bits of things as she helped carry trays in from the kitchen and the only things that were any good were the crisps and salted peanuts and the sausages on sticks. Garlic butter was foul, gherkins were all sour and watery, and salami was full of fatty white lumps. She couldn't eat crab patties because of crabs, like lobsters, being plunged into boiling water, olives were slimy and tasted of snot, and the stuffing was so hideously and ghastlily hot that it almost took the roof of your mouth off. She would far rather have had jellies and trifles and pink-iced cakes any day of the week, she didn't care if they *were* ordinary and childish. She supposed that just went to show, what Rose was so often telling her: 'You haven't any sophistication . . . none whatsoever.'

At ten past six the first gaggle of guests arrived, having met up at Victoria Station and travelled on the same train. Nicola could hear them coming when they were still only half way down the road: their voices, like Rose's, were peculiarly penetrating and shrill. Everybody had brought a birthday present. They were the sort of presents that grown-ups gave each other – bottles of scent and jars of bath crystals – which Nicola wouldn't have looked twice at, but which Rose appeared delighted with, at any rate if the amount of gush was anything to go by.

'*Susie*, that's *super*! That's just what I *wanted* . . . isn't it *gorgeous*? Doesn't it smell *super*? I just can't *wait* to put some on.'

On the other hand, Rose and her friends were always gushing so perhaps it didn't mean anything. One girl had brought a pair of blue dangly earrings which needed pierced ears. She cried out in amazement when Rose said she'd never had her ears pierced.

'*Haven't* you? I had mine done *ages* ago.'

Rose instantly became mad to have her ears pierced straight away. Mrs Bruce said, 'We'll see. Perhaps for Christmas.' Nicola could tell, from the expression on Rose's face – lips pursed so tight that they almost turned in on themselves – that she had not the least intention of waiting till Christmas. Christmas was eight long months off: when Rose said straight away she meant *now*.

At a quarter past six Denny arrived, and soon after that another bunch of Ida Johnsonites, who had also come from Victoria but by a different train. In Rose's class at Ida Johnson there were twelve girls and twelve boys. Rose had invited all of the girls and four of the boys. Like Mrs Bruce, she didn't really care very much for boys. The four she had invited struck Nicola as being rather sappy. They had sappy names, for a start. One was Anthony, one was Conrad, one was Wayne and one was Alastair. Unlike Denny, who had come in Levis and a sweater, they were all wearing shirts, and proper trousers with creases. Anthony even had a spotted bow tie. Probably all of the other boys in Rose's class were quite normal, ordinary boys who wore denims and trainers and kicked footballs, but then Rose wouldn't invite normal, ordinary boys; she would think they were rough and uncouth, as Mrs Bruce did.

All the girls were pretty and shrieking, just like Rose. They all had very long, thick hair, either dead straight as if it had been ironed, or very curly and bouncy, except for one girl who had a frizz, like bits of wire, which she said had just been done for her by 'Mr Marcus'. Everyone stood round saying, 'Gosh, it's *super*,' and, 'Gosh, you are *brave*,' and 'Gosh, d'you think it'd suit *me*?' Nicola, who privately thought it looked hideous, was incensed when Mrs Bruce said: 'That's exactly what Nicola needs doing to hers . . . give it a bit of body.'

'Hope you don't,' whispered Denny.

'You must be *joking*,' said Nicola.

Mr Bruce, who wasn't good at parties, had gone down the garden and locked himself away into his shed with his fretsaw and his electric drill and his old tobacco tins full of assorted nails. Ben, because his manners were bad and he couldn't be trusted not to get up on his hind legs and help himself to sausages and crab patties, not to mention knocking over people's drinks every time he wagged his tail, had been banished to the kitchen with a fresh marrow bone. Mrs Bruce hovered in the doorway, as if she couldn't quite make up her mind whether to go or whether to stay. Rose had introduced her as 'My big sister', and everyone had laughed, including Mrs Bruce, who had said 'Get away with you!' and looked pleased. Nicola was introduced as, 'My *other* sister, who does ballet.' Someone said: 'Are you going to be a dancer?'

'Don't know yet,' said Nicola.

'Of course you are!' Mrs Bruce bustled forward with another bottle of chilled apple juice. 'She's got an audition to Kendra Hall.'

'Yes, but I haven't *passed* it yet.'

'Well, even if you don't . . . there are other places.'

She wasn't sure that she would want other places; not if she failed Kendra Hall.

'I couldn't bear to do an *ordinary* job,' said the someone who had asked if she were going to be a dancer. 'Could you?'

The question was addressed not so much to Nicola as to the room in general. There was a chorus of '*Ugh*'s and '*Yuck*'s, and Rose's voice rising clear above the hubbub: 'I'd sooner *die* than not be able to act.' The first girl said, 'Me *too*' and all rest nodded their heads and made vigorous noises in agreement. Nicola had heard the cry so often that it no longer made any impression on her. Denny, however, was obviously struck by it.

'That's daft,' he said.

Everyone stopped nodding and turned to look at him.

'*Typical*,' said the girl with the frizz. 'Absolutely *typical*.'

'It's what comes of not being in the business,' said Rose. (She and her friends, and Mrs Bruce, always referred to the theatre as 'the business': it was either the business or 'the profession'.) 'Ordinary people just don't understand.'

'Don't understand what?' said Denny.

'That once you've been in it, there's literally *nothing* else that you can do.'

'*Nothing*,' said the girl with the frizzy hair.

A ripple of irritation passed across Denny's forehead.

'That's crap,' he said.

'It's not crap!' The girl with the frizz was beginning to bristle. 'It's what's called dedication.'

'I don't call it dedication,' said Denny. 'I call it stupid. Saying there's nothing else you can do . . . there's always *some*thing people can do.'

'Like what?'

'Like washing up cups and saucers . . . anyone could do that.'

'I'd rather *die*!' said Rose.

'Bet you wouldn't,' said Denny. 'Not if it came to it. I

bet if it came to it and someone said all right, I'll stick a needle in you and then you can die sooner than wash up cups and saucers, I bet you'd sooner wash up cups and saucers. Sooner than let 'em stick a needle in you.'

'I wouldn't *have* to let them.' Rose made the statement grandly, in her best dramatic fashion. 'There wouldn't be any need. . . . If I couldn't act,' said Rose, 'I should already *be* dead without anyone sticking needles in me.'

The girl with the frizzy hair said, 'That's *it*.'

'So there,' said Rose.

Nicola wondered yet again why it was that Rose always seemed to have the last word. Even when you knew she wasn't right you could never think of a come-back – not, at any rate, until hours later, when you'd unravelled all the strands of the argument and discovered where it was that she had hoodwinked you.

After the buffet supper had been demolished, and everyone had said how super the lobster patties were and how champagne was the most gorgeous drink in the world, Rose, in her bossy way, announced that they were all going to play *Don't Say a Word* and that she and Frizzy Hair (who turned out to be Susie Siegenberg, who was the girl who thought she was a second Barbra Streisand and suffered from terrible raging jealousy) were going to pick teams. Denny and Nicola, because nobody knew them, were the last to be picked, which meant that they weren't together. Rose had Denny, because, 'I can't pick my own *sister*,' and Susie Siegenberg had Nicola.

'Nicola's good at mime,' said Rose.

It wasn't very often that Rose handed out the compliments. Nicola felt a glow of pride, and then felt cross with herself: it was only *Rose*. Still, even it it were only Rose it would be nice to show all these screaming friends of hers that other people beside themselves could do things. She heard Denny saying that he didn't know what the game was about, and Rose saying impatiently that he could pick it up as they went along, and then she was swept off into a corner with the rest of her team to think up phrases for the other side to mime.

'They've all got to be theatrical,' said Susie.

Nobody disputed that, so Nicola didn't bother arguing even though she'd just thought of a phrase that wasn't theatrical that would have been nice to give Rose ('A pig in a poke' . . . she would like to see Rose mime a pig). Someone said *The Mousetrap*, and someone else said, *Midsummer Night's Dream*.

'*Puss in Boots*.'

'*Babes in the Wood*.'

They managed to think of eight and then got stuck.

'What about Rumpelstiltskin?' said Nicola.

'That's not theatrical!'

'It is sort of.'

'No, it's not, it's a fairy tale.'

'Yes, but it would be fun. You could do rumple, like rumpling hair, and stilt, like walking on stilts, and –'

'*Hamlet*,' said Susie. 'That'll do. I'll tell them we're ready.'

Once, a long time ago, before she had started ballet with Mrs French, Nicola had almost been in a mime show, playing the part of a Bad Little Girl. She *would* have been in it, if it hadn't been for Rose. Rose had screamed and yelled almost non-stop for a whole week, until in the end the part had had to be taken away from Nicola and given to Rose instead. It was something that Nicola had never forgotten, but in spite of that she still enjoyed doing mime.

When it came to her turn she was given *Simple Spymen*, which Rose said was the title of a play. Nicola turned to her side, who had to do the guessing.

'Title of play: two words.'

That was as much as she was allowed to say. All the rest had to be in dumb show. She held up one finger to show that she was about to mime the first word, 'simple'. Simple was simple: she simply drooped her head, stuck her thumb in her mouth and turned in her toes. Everybody laughed.

The boy called Wayne said, 'Daft!'

Nicola shook her head.

'Stupid?'

'Slow.'

'Half wit?'

It wasn't long before someone hit on the correct word. She nodded, to show that they could stop guessing. Now she had to do Spymen. She decided to break it into syllables. First she made chopping motions on her right arm with the fingers of her left hand, which was the sign that meant 'breaking into syllables'; then she held up two fingers to indicate that there were two of them.

Spy was easy. She opened an imaginary door, glanced furtively this way and that, checking that the coast was clear, slipped inside (taking care to close the door very quietly behind her), crept on tiptoe down some steps, knelt at the bottom and peered with one eye through an imaginary keyhole. Two or three people shouted 'Spy!' almost immediately.

'Men' was a bit more difficult. She could have done the classical mime Mrs French had taught her, simply running the flat of her hand down her face and bringing it to a point to indicate a beard, which was what you did in ballet, but that would have seemed like cheating and anyway wasn't very inventive. She wondered for a moment if she dared do something rude and naughty, but thought she'd better not (Mrs Bruce had come to

66

watch) and before she could think of anything else Susie Siegenberg had shouted '*Simple Spymen*!' and it was over.

'One minute thirty seconds,' said Rose, who was timing them with her new birthday watch, which was digital and had lots of clever gadgets such as an alarm bell and a calendar. 'That mean's your side's taken twenty minutes and ten seconds in all. Ours has taken eighteen, and one to go. So if we get the last one in less than two minutes and ten seconds we've won and we get the prize.'

'What prize?' said Nicola. She hadn't heard anything about prizes.

Rose looked round slyly at Mrs Bruce.

'Everyone who's in the winning team has a glass of sherry.'

Mrs Bruce raised an eyebrow. Rose sometimes *was* allowed a sip of sherry as a special treat (Nicola didn't care for it) but a sip was not quite the same thing as a glass. Rose was testing, seeing how far she could go, trusting her mother not to say 'no' in front of people.

'Maybe just a thimbleful,' said Mrs Bruce.

Honour was satisfied. Rose turned back, triumphant, to her team.

'Two minutes nine seconds and not a second more!'

It was unfortunate that the burden of being last should fall on Denny. Nicola could see, just looking at him, that he had already gone all stiff and shy.

The mime he was given was *The Mousetrap*.

'Play.' Denny announced stolidly. 'It's got two words and the first one's "the".'

Squeals from his own side: howls of rage from the other.

'You're not allowed to *say*!'

'You have to make a sign for "the",' said Nicola. She doubled her fist. 'Like that.'

Mutinously, Denny stuck out his lower lip. He doubled his fist and Rose said, '*The*' and then, 'Now do the second word,' all pompous and schoolmistressy as if she were talking to a child. Denny rolled an anguished eye at Nicola: obligingly she made chopping motions on her arm. Susie Siegenberg screeched, 'Don't help him!' and Mrs Bruce, over by the door, said sharply, 'Nicola! That's not fair.'

Nicola sat back, disgruntled. What did she mean, not fair? What wasn't *fair* was expecting Denny to get up and play a game he'd never played before in front of a roomful of people who all went to stage school and had egos the size of giant puffballs. No wonder he wasn't doing it right. People who enjoyed showing off never seemed to realize what an ordeal it was for people who didn't.

Denny, having reluctantly made chopping motions to indicate that we was breaking the word into syllables, was now, even more reluctantly, acting out the first one, jumping across the room with his hands held up in front of him. His team were plainly puzzled.

'Kangaroo,' said Rose.

Nicola's team exploded. Nicola said, 'Kangaroo isn't a syllable,' but no one took any notice of her. Denny went on jumping, his team went on guessing.

'Wallaby?'

'*Rabbit*.'

'Elephant!'

Denny, goaded, said: 'Elephants don't jump.'

'No talking!' screamed Susie Siegenberg.

Rose was growing cross. 'If you can't do the first one, you'd better do the second – and do it *properly*.'

'I *am* doing it properly!'

'You're not, you keep talking.'

Denny scowled.

'*Honestly*,' said Rose. '*Amateurs*.'

'Now, now,' said Mrs Bruce. 'None of that, we can't all be talented.' To Denny, kindly, she said: 'Don't let them upset you. You just get on and do it in your own way.'

Denny's idea of miming the word trap was hardly very inspired, Nicola had to admit it. All he did, awkwardly, because he was self-concsious, was leap in the air and clap his hands together. He did it so fast that his team were left blinking.

'What's that supposed to be?' said Rose angrily.

Denny opened his mouth.

'Don't *talk*.'

'Do it again.'

'And do it so we can *see*.'

For a second time Denny leapt into the air and clapped his hands together. Susie Siegenberg and one or two of the others started giggling. Rose, red in the face, shouted: 'You're not *doing* anything!' Someone said, 'He's jumping again,' and even some of Denny's own team collapsed into giggles.

'But what's it supposed to *be*?'

'That's what you're supposed to be finding out,' said Nicola.

'Do something else! Do it in a different way!'

Denny did try. He got down on his knees and crawled about the carpet, then suddenly clamped his hand over a bright red flower that was part of the pattern. Someone said, 'Kill!'

'*Bang*.'

'Squash – '

'Flat – '

'*Time*!' Susie Siegenberg gave a shrill screech of triumph. 'Two minutes and eleven seconds ... that means we've won!'

Rose, deprived both of her sherry and the honour and

glory, was by now bright scarlet.

'That's what comes of using amateurs. They're just so stupid . . . I *loathe* them.'

There were times when Nicola felt so ashamed of being related to Rose that it almost hurt. Mrs Bruce had already gone out to the kitchen to fetch the promised thimblefuls of sherry for the winning side, or she might at least have made her apologize. Everyone said that Mrs Bruce spoiled Rose, but even she wouldn't tolerate rudeness to guests.

Nicola left her seat and went over to Denny.

'Want to come and take Ben for a walk?'

Denny shrugged a shoulder.

'Can if you like.'

'It'd be better than staying here,' said Nicola.

As they reached the door, Rose's voice came shrieking after them: 'Where are you two going?'

'Mind your own business,' said Nicola.

In the hall they bumped into Mrs Bruce, bearing a tray with six tiny little glasses and three egg cups filled with sherry.

'It's all right,' she said, 'I've got everything. Who won in the end?'

'We did,' said Nicola. 'But I don't want any sherry, we're going to take Ben out.'

'But the party isn't finished yet.'

'Don't care,' said Nicola. 'I don't want to stay any more.'

For a moment she thought her mother was going to start lecturing her on bad manners ('Walking out of your sister's own birthday party!') but she only shook her head and said, 'Well, don't go too far, I want you back here before it's dark – and don't go over that Common!'

They collected Ben from the kitchen and went out

round the side of the house.

'Where we going?' said Denny.

'Anywhere.' Anywhere that took them away from ghastly Rose. 'Let's go to your place and show Ben to your mother.'

'All right.'

For a long while they walked in silence, the only sounds being the happy snuffling of Ben's nose as he investigated smells along the way. Nicola was still feeling too embarrassed for conversation. Sometimes, like when she saw Rose on stage, she felt almost proud to have her for a sister; other times, like now, she felt she would do anything to have a sister who was plain and quiet and ordinary, and *didn't* run around shrieking and making a noise and always having to be the centre of attention. Obviously Denny didn't feel much like talking, either, because it wasn't until they reached the outskirts of his estate that he said anything.

'I suppose,' he said, glumly, 'you'll get like that when you go to this ballet school.'

Nicola didn't ask him what he meant by 'like that': she knew well enough.

'I jolly well will *not*,' she said; and then, as an afterthought: 'Anyway, I haven't got there yet.'

6

The audition had been fixed for April 24th, which was the week after Easter. Term ended ten days earlier, on April 14th, amidst the usual flurry of exams and inter-house competitions. St Mary's Streatham had four houses, Tudor, Windsor, Stuart and York. Nicola was in Stuart, whose colour was a nice bright scarlet (Windsor's was a wishy-washy blue, York was egg-sick yellow, and Tudor pea-puke green). Last year she had played left wing for the under-fourteen hockey XI, which had swept the board, beating all the others hollow. This year she was supposed to have been playing for the under-fifteens, and at the beginning of term had even been elected captain, only Miss Camfield, quite nicely but nonetheless firmly, had said she didn't think it was a good idea to have a captain who might not always be available to play, so Linda Baker had ended up doing it instead. Now Miss Camfield was justified, because in this, the most crucial match of all, the interhouse final between Stuart and Tudor, Nicola had to drop out and give way to the reserve. Miss Camfield shook her head and said that of course she understood but it really did seem a shame when Nicola had worked so hard and the team had been doing so well.

'In my experience it's always fatal to break up a win-ning team, it upsets the whole balance. Still, if it's really important – '

She looked at Nicola hopefully as she spoke. Just for a moment Nicola was tempted. It *was* important; certainly it was important. It was the most important event of her life so far. On the other hand there was still almost a fortnight to go, and she wasn't *very* likely to sustain any ghastly injury just playing a game of hockey. Janice Martin last year had admittedly tripped over and broken her ankle, which had meant having her foot in plaster for weeks on end, but then Janice Martin was the clumsy sort of person who did things like that. Nicola wasn't clumsy.

'I suppose you couldn't possibly . . . .'

Miss Camfield let the words trail off. She knew that Nicola couldn't possibly: so in her heart of hearts did Nicola. If you were going to be a dancer, you had to make sacrifices; she had accepted that a long time ago. It still didn't make it any easier to bear, having to sit on the sidelines and watch while Janice Martin played left wing in her place. Janice Martin had improved since last year, when she had been clumsy enough to trip over her own feet. She actually made the pass which enabled Sarah, playing centre forward, to score the winning goal. *That* made it even less easy to bear. Naturally she was glad that Stuart had won, but it was hard not to feel a pang as everyone rushed round congratulating Janice Martin when they could have been congratulating her. She had to remind herself, very firmly, that hockey was only a game: ballet was a vocation. Hadn't Rose and her mother told her so a million times? Unfortunately, when she heard Miss Camfield also congratulating Janice Martin ('If you play as well as that next year you should make one of the school teams') it didn't help as much as it probably ought to have done. Horrid jealousy *would* persist in raising its head.

End-of-term exam results were read out and Nicola

had come top in biology again, which made everyone groan.

'It gets to be so *boring*,' said Sarah.

Miss Richardson looked at her sharply.

'If you think it's so boring, then the solution is in your own hands . . . work a bit harder and Nicola might get some competition.' Afterwards, to Nicola, as she handed back the papers, she said: 'That was excellent, Nicola. You'll see that at the bottom I've written *Keep up the good work*, but on second thoughts I don't think that's necessary . . . you'll keep it up anyway. Good girl!' And then, half turning as she moved away: 'I have very high hopes for you, you know.'

Next morning Miss Camfield read out the overall class results. A girl called Denise Marshall, who had an IQ of about a thousand, had come top, while Nicola shared second place with Denny. She was so pleased about her and Denny being bracketed together that she almost forgot to be pleased about coming second – she almost forgot that she *had* come second, until Miss Camfield, unexpectedly, reminded her of it.

'With results like these, Nicola,' she said, 'it does seem a terrible waste applying for ballet school.'

Nicola was indignant. Why did it seem a waste?

'It's a waste because you could be doing something else,' said Denny, as they walked home together that evening.

'Like what?'

'Like being a nuclear physicist, or something.'

'I don't want to be a nuclear physicist!'

'Well, or a doctor or something. 'Stead of just a brainless dancer.'

She rounded on him.

'Who said dancers are brainless?'

'I did.'

'Well, they're not! *I'm* not.'

'That's why you should be doing something else.'

Nicola frowned: they seemed to be going in circles.

'Don't see what's so wonderful about having brains anyway.'

'Don't wear out like bodies.'

'They do! Miss Richardson says your brain cells start dying the minute you're born.'

'Yeah, but people can still use 'em,' said Denny. 'Even when they're old. They don't get worn out by the time you're fifty, like legs and arms and that.'

That was true. Nicola thought of her grandfather, who could still read books and do his beloved jumbo crosswords every day even though his arthritis was so bad he could sometimes hardly walk. She wondered what Rose would do when she was as old as that and had arthritis. Sit in front of the video, probably, watching all her old TV shows and her commercials for Dreamy Liquid. She giggled.

'What're you laughing at?' said Denny.

She told him of her vision of Rose. Denny took it seriously and said, 'That's the sort of thing that happens when people don't have any brain.'

'Rose has got a brain . . . she just doesn't use it.'

'So that's what happens when people don't use it. You coming down the club to play table tennis tonight?'

Nicola shook her head, regretfully.

'I can't tonight, I've got an extra class with Mrs French.'

'What about tomorrow?'

'Tomorrow I've got to stay on at school . . . it's the dress rehearsal for the show.'

Denny made a noise of disgust.

'S'pose you won't be able to come swimming on Saturday, either?'

'Not just before the show,' said Nicola.

The St Mary's end-of-term show was always something special. This term it was even more special than usual: a punk-rock opera, composed by the senor music group, with the help of Mr Forbes, who was Head of Music. Nicola had three solos to do (dancing, not singing: she couldn't sing to save her life). They were not exactly the sort of solos she learnt with Mrs French, but perhaps for that very reason they were all the more fun. The one she enjoyed most was the last one, where she dressed up as a punk marionette in a stripey wig of green and purple. Everyone said that it was sure to bring the house down.

'What about the Saturday after?' said Denny. 'S'pose you'll tell me you can't do it then because of the audition?'

'It'll be all right *after* the audition.' After the audition she would be able to do anything he wanted her to do – go swimming, play table tennis, even climb mountains if he could find any for her to climb. 'It's just that until that's over – '

'Until that's *over*,' said Denny, with heavy sarcasm, 'I'm surprised you're even allowed to just *walk*.'

Rose couldn't come to the end-of-term show because she was spending that weekend with a girl from Ida Johnson called Kathy Wilson (the one who had given her the earrings). She quite often did spend weekends with Kathy Wilson. Mrs Bruce had once said, only half jokingly, that she didn't know why she just didn't pack her bags and go and live there. Kathy Wilson, on the other hand, never spent weekends with Rose, because, as Rose was for ever explaining, 'the Wilsons' home was more exciting than the Bruces'.

'It's got a swimming pool, and a tennis court, and a

real viewing room for showing films . . . that's why it's best for me to go round there.'

Since Rose was round there so often it might have been thought she could have postponed this one particular visit until the following week, but Mrs Bruce didn't suggest it and Nicola wouldn't lower herself. When Rose, making her eyes go all big, said, 'Gosh, I'm *ever* so sorry! I wouldn't have said I'd go if I'd realized,' Nicola just shrugged her shoulders and pretended not to care.

'Doesn't matter, it's only some tatty school thing. Not professional.'

'Yes, but even *so*,' said Rose.

There was a pause.

'I s'pose I could always ring Kathy and tell her I can't come.'

'Honestly,' said Nicola, 'it doesn't matter.' She only said it because she knew that if she took her up on the offer Rose would sulk and resent it. What Rose liked was to make magnanimous gestures without actually having to follow them through.

'But you are my *sister*,' said Rose.

'Well – ' Nicola hesitated. If Rose really did mean it, for once –

'But then p'raps her parents might think it was a bit rude . . . I mean, accepting an invitation and then ringing up at the last moment. I promised I'd take my video of *Children of the New Forest* for them. They never saw me in that. I said I'd take it with me so we could watch it. I s'pose I could always give it to Kathy in class tomorrow. The only trouble is, she's so forgetful. She'd probably leave it on the train or something . . . I do feel *awful*. You ought to have reminded me.'

Rose shouldn't have needed any reminding, the date had been ringed in red felt-tip on the kitchen calendar

77

for weeks past. There simply wasn't any excuse. Nicola would never have dreamt of not turning up for one of Rose's performances. (There would have been the most tremendous scene if she *had*.)

'Anyway,' said Rose, comfortably, 'you're only doing a couple of numbers.'

'Three, actually,' said Nicola.

'Yes, but I mean, it's not as if you're the star turn or anything. I mean, obviously I'd come *then*, even if it did mean being rude to Kathy's parents.'

Oh, obviously, thought Nicola. Obviously, indubitably, and without any doubt.

'It's not like when I was in *The March Girls*,' said Rose, growing happy. 'I mean, I know I wasn't the *star*, exactly, but it was in the West End, and I did have my picture outside the theatre, and I did have a write-up in *The Stage*. D'you remember that write-up in *The Stage*? What was it they said? Something about Amy being irresistible –'

Rose knew perfectly well what it was that *The Stage* had said. Nicola wasn't going to pander to her vanity by repeating it.

'Really,' she said, 'it was so long ago I can't even remember what you did in it.'

'I sang that song! The Amy song! *How fine to be pretty* –' Rose promptly put on her Amy expression (a revolting simper) and began to do her little Amy dance about the room, singing lustily as she went: '*How fine to be pretty, And witty, And cute! How fine to me me – Ah, me! A-my!* . . . surely you remember?'

Nicola made a vague, grudging, mumbling sound.

'You *must* do,' said Rose. 'I wore that plaid dress with the yellow sash – I've still got it upstairs. I'll go and get it down and show you. *Then* you'll remember.'

Nicola comforted herself with the reflection that Rose

was one of those people who was just naturally selfish. There probably wasn't anything she could do about it. It was like having pimply arms or thick ankles: if that was the way you were, then that was the way you were.

Even if Rose didn't come to the show, everybody else did. Mr and Mrs French came, and Denny and his family, and of course Nicola's own parents. Mr Bruce wanted to know if he should bring earplugs or whether they would be provided. Nicola thought at first that he was being serious: it took her a moment or so to realize that he was only teasing.

'It's not as loud as all *that*,' she said.

The opera was called *Snow White and the Seven Gorillas*. Snow White was played by a black girl from Class 5 called Leonora Dacey. The special arts group had designed her a silvery punk wig cut in Mohican style, and she had painted her face dead white like a mask. The seven gorillas were the seven hugest and most hulking boys in the school, dressed in frayed knee-length jeans held up by braces, thick-soled boots, and a whole armoury of padlocks and chains. On their bare chests were stuck what looked like hairy rugs dyed all colours of the rainbow, pink and mauve and brightest orange. Everybody laughed when they came clumping on, but although the jokes fell thick and fast the real aim was to make people think, because the gorillas turned out not to be anywhere near as funny as they seemed. At the end of the opera they suddenly discovered that under her paint and her silvery wig Snow White wasn't white at all, and instead of competing with each other for her favours they all banded together and organized a march saying BLACKS OUT. After they had thumped across the stage with their BLACKS OUT banners they reappeared with banners saying JEWS OUT; and then after JEWS OUT

they had banners saying PEOPLE FROM YORKSHIRE OUT, and PYGMIES OUT, and DOWN WITH PEOPLE WHO WEAR GLASSES and SQUASH THE OVER-NINETIES and KILL ALL THE ANTS, so that by the time the curtain came down even the dumbest member of the audience would surely have got the message.

Nicola's punk marionette was one of the show-stoppers. It was called *Dance of a Lost Soul* and was funny but sad and serious too, which people obviously appreciated because although at first they laughed they gradually fell quite silent, not even coughing or shuffling or rustling their programmes, until the final moment of collapse, when the puppet master let fall the strings and the puppet slowly crumpled into a heap. Then the clapping started; slowly to begin with, but gathering momentum like a tidal wave. People clapped and clapped until their hands must have been sore.

Nicola had never been applauded like that before. Everyone, afterwards, seemed to want to congratulate her. Miss Richardson came up, looking most unusually smart (and very feminine, Nicola was pleased to observe: she hoped that Denny had seen and taken note) in a matching skirt and jacket, and a silk blouse with big floppy collar. Generally one only ever saw her in her white lab. coat. She said, 'That was excellent, Nicola! I knew you did ballet, but I never realized you could dance like that.'

Mr French tapped his camera and told her that he had 'Got some good ones here . . . you just wait till you see 'em!' Mrs French, all smiles, said that it was fun to let one's hair down occasionally, Mrs Bruce kept explaining to perfect strangers that 'That's my older daughter, the one that did the marionette dance . . . my younger one's at Ida Johnson. This one's got an audition for Kendra Hall.'

Various members of Class 3 rushed round shrieking 'Where's Nicola? Where's Nicola?' Sarah dragged her off to meet a cousin who was 'mad about ballet and wants to talk to a real dancer'; Cheryl could be heard yelling that 'That's Nicola, over there . . . she's one of my best friends!' Linda Baker, in her bossy self-important fashion, wanted her to 'Come and be introduced to my auntie,' even Janice Martin, who knew all there was to know, condescendingly allowed the marionette dance to have been 'quite good'.

'Not really *ballet*, of course, but quite good all the same.'

A girl from Class 6, who had never before addressed so much as a single word to Nicola, except perhaps to yell at her for talking when she shouldn't, or for not walking in single file when she should have been, came up and said, 'That was great! It's about time we had some real talent in this place.' Even Miss Camfield, peeved though she was about ballet taking priority over hockey and gym, had something nice to say. The only person who hadn't was Denny. Denny didn't say anything at all, for the simple reason that he wasn't there. She knew he *had* been there, because she had seen him sitting in the second row with his mother and sisters, but he didn't come backstage and he was nowhere to be found in either the hall or the main corridor, where lots of people were still gathered. Surely, she thought, he couldn't be so mean as to have gone home without waiting for her?

Just for a moment all the lovely brightness threatened to cloud over, but then she turned and saw Mr Barnes, the Head of the Music Department. He was talking to Mr Henry, who was the Head Master, and was nodding in Nicola's direction as he did so. Nicola caught his eye and quickly looked away, in case he thought that she was try-

82

ing to eavesdrop. (But Mr Barnes and Mr Henry talking about *her*?)

'This is our young dancer.' (They had been! They were coming towards her.) 'Even did some of the choreography herself, from what I'm told.'

'Really?' Mr Henry beamed. 'So she's a choreographer as well as a ballerina, eh?'

Nicola blushed and did her best to look modest. (She didn't like to correct Mr Henry and tell him that ballerina was a special rank reserved only for the top few, like a prima donna in opera. It was funny how people seemed to think you could refer to any type of dancer, even the least important member of the corps de ballet, as a ballerina. They would never dream of calling an ordinary soldier a general.)

'A splendid job,' said Mr Henry. 'The local paper came, you know. I daresay there'll be a write-up. There'll certainly be one in the school magazine, I can give you my word on that!'

Beaming and nodding, he went on his way, accompanied by Mr French. Sarah, who had been hovering a few feet off, now came buzzing forward, all excited, to whisper: 'I just heard Miss Camfield telling someone that "that's the girl who's going to go to ballet school and be a dancer", and the person she was talking to said, "I'm not surprised, she's got a real touch of quality" . . . quality!' Sarah gloated. 'I bet no one ever said that about Rose.'

They might have done, thought Nicola; but anyway it wasn't as if she was in any sort of competition. She'd never wanted to be *better* than Rose.

'Nicola!' Her mother was beckoning to her, making signs that it was time to go. Nicola tore herself away with some reluctance. She could have stayed on a lot longer, listening to all the comments (and receiving words of praise) but Mr Bruce would have had enough. He had never been a great one for going backstage or hanging around after a performance. Neither had Nicola in the old days, when it had been Rose who had been receiving all the praise. She wondered if that meant that deep down in the depths of herself, she was a rather nasty, attention-seeking person. She didn't *think* that she was, but then Rose probably didn't think that she was vain and selfish; it was only other people who thought so.

'Well!' said Mr Bruce, as they left school by the main gates and turned towards the High Street. 'That was a turn up for the books.'

Turn up for the books? What did that mean?

'A pity our Rosie wasn't there . . . might have given her something to think about!'

'I do wish,' said Mrs Bruce, 'that you wouldn't call her Rosie.'

'What's a turn up for the books?' said Nicola.

'It means your father was pleasantly surprised. I've kept telling him it's right for you to go to ballet school; now perhaps he'll believe me.'

'Well, I'm certainly impressed, I don't mind admitting that. Mind you –'

'There's Denny!' Nicola leapt forward. He hadn't gone off without her after all: he was waiting on the corner of the road, by the National Westminster Bank. She might have known he wouldn't really have gone home without saying something.

'I've bin here for ages,' he said, as she ran up to him. 'I began to think you weren't ever going to come.'

'So why didn't you wait?'

'I did wait, I told you, I've bin waiting for ages!'

'No, but at *school!*'

Denny pulled a face. She looked at him, frowning. 'What's that s'posed to mean?'

'You were behaving like Rose,' said Denny.

'I was not!' She was outraged. How could *anyone*, *ever*, accuse her of behaving like Rose? Rose, who shrieked and ran about gushing? Nicola had never run about gushing in her life. 'I wasn't behaving a *bit* like Rose!'

'Yes, you were . . . just like.'

Denny always stuck doggedly to any point that he had made. That was because he didn't usually make one without first having given it serious consideration. Had she *really* been behaving like Rose?

She heard herself screaming across a crowd of people at Cheryl, saw herself simpering at Mr French, basking in the approval of Mr Henry, listening enraptured as people told her how wonderful she was . . . .

'You were enjoying it,' said Denny.

He sounded accusing. Nicola felt suddenly cross.

'Why shouldn't I enjoy it?' It was nice to be told that you were talented. Anyone would enjoy it – even Denny.

They stomped along for a while in silence. From some way behind came her mother's voice: 'You mind you stick to the main road! I don't want you going over that Common.'

If was offputting, having parents trailing you only a hundred yards behind. You couldn't hold hands with parents there. In a small voice, Nicola said: 'Didn't you like it?'

'Yeah, I thought it was great.'

'But didn't you like *me*?'

'Course I did,' said Denny.

'So why didn't you *say* something?'

'Didn't need me telling you,' said Denny. 'Not with everybody else doing it.'

7

On the Monday after school had broken up, Nicola's report arrived in its familiar brown envelope. It came while the family were still at breakfast, which was rather embarrassing because Mr Bruce slit open the envelope there and then (the first time he had ever done such a thing) and, having skimmed through the contents, proceeded to read them out so that everyone could hear.

'*English* . . . Nicola has worked extremely well this term. *French* . . . she shows a good grasp of the language. *Computer Studies* . . . has taken an intelligent interest. *Maths* . . . Nicola is not a mathematician but has achieved a respectable result through sheer determination and hard work. *Physical Education* . . . a naturally gifted athlete. *Music* . . . applies herself well and has a good ear. *Biology* . . . an excellent term's work. Nicola should go far in this subject. *Needlework* – '

Needlework wasn't very good. Mrs Hibbert complained that she didn't take the subject seriously and made 'scant effort to overcome natural deficiencies'. Rose, sarcastic, said: 'Glad to know she's *got* some natural deficiencies.' Nicola didn't blame her. If anyone had read out a report like that on Rose she would have felt like vomiting all across the table. Of course she was happy to hear nice things said about herself, but after Denny's accusations of Saturday she was being extra specially careful not to show it. She just turned a bit pink and mushed her muesli about with a spoon and made a few mumbling noises.

'S'pose you think you're too clever for needlework,' said Rose.

'If she did, it would be very silly.' Mrs Bruce spoke briskly, nodding at Nicola over the teapot as she did so. 'It's never clever to be impractical.'

'I'm not impractical,' said Nicola. She might not be able to sew in a straight line or do lazy daisy stitch to save her life, but she could make things out of pieces of wood and she could put model kits together and she could do fretsaw work. She could even mend fuses and knew how to change washers on taps, which was more than Rose did. 'You'll find a knowledge of needlework comes in very handy,' said Mrs Bruce. 'You won't always have dressers running round after you ready to take up hems and put tucks in things.'

'Not unless you get to be a star,' said Rose.

'What about this biology, then?' Mr Bruce tapped a finger against the report.

'What about it?' said Mrs Bruce.

'Isn't this the woman that takes them for physics and what-have-you later on?'

'She takes the fourth years,' said Nicola. 'Miss Khan takes you after that.'

'Who's Miss Khan?' Rose wanted to know.

'She was new last term. It used to be Mr Gorringe, he was horrible. Now it's Miss Khan. She's super.'

Nicola had been looking forward to reaching the fifth year and doing physics and chemistry with Miss Khan – she'd been looking forward to reaching Class 4 and doing it with Miss Richardson, as well. She reminded herself, just in time, that in all probability she still *would* be doing it. It wasn't in the least likely that she would be accepted for Kendra Hall.

'Eighty-two per cent,' said Mr Bruce. 'That's a pretty good mark.'

'She always gets that in biology. A pity she can't work as hard at things like needlework and domestic science . . . those scones she brought home the other day were like lead pellets.'

Rose giggled.

'D'you remember that time she put the sugar in the oven to dry and it all went and melted?'

'Yes, I do,' said Mrs Bruce. 'I also remember the time she kindly scrubbed a polished table for me with bleach.'

'That was when I was *five*!' said Nicola.

'Yes, well, in some respects I'd say you hadn't changed much. Anyone who can wilfully cut holes in a perfectly good carpet – '

'I didn't *wil*fully.'

The carpet was a sore point. It was Nicola's bedroom carpet, and it wasn't as good as all that; it had threadbare patches in the middle and was starting to fray at the edges. It was the fraying which had caused all the trouble, because the frayed bits kept catching in the doors of her bookcase (proper glass-fronted doors: the bookcase was Victorian, and she had inherited it from a great aunt). Cutting away a tiny piece of carpet had seemed at the time the obvious solution. She saw now that it wasn't, but she hadn't seen it *then*, so it could hardly be called wilful. And anyway, that had been almost three months ago. You'd have thought it could have been forgotten about by now.

'Who's this Miss Camfield?' said Mr Bruce.

'She's my class teacher.'

'According to her, Nicola is a sensible and responsible girl who is an asset to the school community.'

Rose made a cackling sound, like a goose. Mrs Bruce

said, 'Sensible! She obviously doesn't know what she's like with carpets. Nicola, why are you messing that muesli around?'

'I don't *like* muesli.' Horrid, nasty, chewy stuff.

'You just eat it up, it's good for you.'

'It's hateful. I don't want it.' She pushed her plate away. 'I've got to go out, anyhow. I'm meeting Denny.'

'Why?' said Mrs Bruce. 'Where are you going?'

'We're going up to Earl's Court, there's a computer exhibition.'

'Well, you make sure you're back in plenty of time to have a rest. You've got a class at five, don't forget.'

She hardly could. She was having classes every day, now, until the audition.

'You be back no later than three. It's tiring, traipsing round exhibitions. You really ought to be staying at home taking things easy for the next few days. In fact – '

Nicola fled. She had promised Denny weeks ago that she would go to the exhibition with him; she wasn't backing out now, audition or no audition.

The great day arrived. Denny, the night before, had somewhat bashfully wished her good luck – 'Hope you get in, if that's what you want.' Rose, in best theatrical tradition, had sent her a card; her father, as he left for work, said: 'Well! So this is it, then? The Day of Reckoning . . . '

The audition was at eleven o'clock, so there was no time to be lost. Before going to bed the previous night Nicola had packed a bag containing all that she would need – one pair of soft shoes, one pair of pointe shoes, leotard, tights, leg warmers in case it was cold, cardigan likewise, band for hair, supply of hair grips. After she

89

had packed it Mrs Bruce had come in and unpacked it again, just to check, 'Because you know you can't be trusted,' but there hadn't been anything missing. Nicola wasn't anywhere near as careless as her mother liked to make out; not when it came to things that mattered.

Mrs French wasn't able to accompany her to the audition because of being pregnant and having to stay in bed a lot of the time. Apparently people didn't always have to stay in bed when they were pregnant; just sometimes, if the baby was misbehaving or threatening to arrive too early, which was what Mrs French's baby was doing.

'I told you,' said Rose, 'it's *hateful*, being pregnant . . . I'm not going to be, *ever*.'

Nicola didn't think it was hateful exactly, but it was certainly a nuisance. It meant that instead of travelling up to town with Mrs French, feeling pleasantly mature and sophisticated, she had to go with her mother and be reduced to the status of a child, and told 'not to sit and frown' and 'remember to go to the toilet on the train because we don't want to have to do it at Victoria'. Nicola didn't like going to the toilet on trains: everyone knew where you were going and what you were going there for. Sometimes, if she simply had to and she was by herself, she would move on, afterwards, to another compartment so that she didn't have to sit there with everyone looking at her, but she could hardly explain that to her mother. Mrs Bruce would only tell her not to be so silly. She had just decided that she would hold herself until she reached Kendra Hall, even if she did feel as if she were bursting, when her mother said: 'We're almost at Victoria. You'd better go, you know what you're like.'

'It's all right,' said Nicola. 'I can wait.'

'That's what you say now . . . we've still got a long tube journey ahead of us. You just do as you're told, and go.'

She knew that if she didn't there would only be an embarrassing scene. Head held high and cheeks flaming she marched out of the compartment. She was glad, afterwards, because the tube journey *was* long (thirteen stops on the district line, all the way out to a place called Ealing Common) but it still didn't soothe the fierce resentment. Treated like a *child*.

They reached Kendra Hall at half past ten. It was just as Mrs French had described it – just as it looked from the photographs in the brochure. It had once been somebody or other's manor house and was full of oak panelling and funny creaky staircases with galleries running round the top. Nicola thought it must be wonderful to live in a house as old as that. All Mrs Bruce said was, 'You'd never keep the dust down.' Imagine worrying about *dust*.

There were eleven other girls besides Nicola taking the audition. Some, like Rose, shrieked a lot and showed off, and talked to one another in loud voices as they changed; others, like Nicola, stayed quite quiet and just got on with the business of smoothing wrinkles out of tights and securing hair with hair grips. Nicola wondered if deep down the ones who shrieked were as nervous as the ones who didn't shriek, or whether there really were people who could come for an audition to a place like Kendra Hall and not feel anything. She herself wasn't actually *paralysed* – Mrs French had told her to 'Take it in your stride, it'll be no different from any ordinary class' – but she couldn't suppress the odd jittery feeling just now and again.

The first jittery feeling was when they were fetched to go up to the studio and found no less than four people waiting for them. One, who was quite young and pretty-ish, was introduced as Miss Flowerdew: she was the one who was to take the class. The other three – a severe-looking elderly lady with gold-rimmed spectacles, a

plump smiling lady in a white coat, and a small spidery man with little dark eyes that darted continually this way and that – sat in a row, like the Inquisition, on hard, high-backed chairs behind a table. Nicola could see that they all had notepads in front of them, and pens at the ready for making notes. She tried to imagine what they would write about her – Nicola Bruce: weak allegro? Poor elevation? Clumsy footwork? Only she wouldn't be Nicola Bruce, she would be number fourteen, because that was what she had been given to pin to her chest. (Fourteen was the same as her age, which could be some kind of omen, though whether good or bad she hadn't yet had time to decide.)

The class, as Mrs French had promised, was very much the same as an ordinary class except for the fact that they were all wearing numbers and being watched like hawks. And try as you might you could never *quite* forget that this was an audition and that Kendra Hall was one of the best ballet schools in the country.

When they came to adage, which Nicola had been looking forward to, she was a bit disappointed, because the steps they were given seemed so simple – *chassé, attitudes croisées, en face, effacées* into *arabesque fondue allongée, pas de bourrée dessus* – they might almost, she thought, have been back in their first year of ballet. And then they came to allegro and that was when she had her second really bad moment of the jitters: the allegro was so fearsomely and hideously complex that she just knew she was never going to get through it. She had time only to think, 'How *unfair*' before the music had started and they were off, *sauté, changement, glissade derrière* . . .

She made it until about three quarters of the way through, when quite suddenly the girl who was numbered fifteen, and who should by rights have been turning diagonally away from Nicola, turned diagonally towards her, so that for one split second their astonished glances met. Rose wouldn't have been thrown, because Rose never was. Even when Rose was wrong (which she had been known to be) she continued regardless. Nicola hesitated for just that split second, and was lost. She picked up again, but her concentration had gone. She didn't exactly disgrace herself, but she could hardly believe that she had come up to the high standards of Kendra Hall. It was true that several other people besides number fifteen had become hopelessly muddled. Nicola hadn't actually turned the wrong way or performed the wrong steps; only just fluffed it a little. Still, there were probably some people who hadn't fluffed it at all.

As they left the studio the girl marked fifteen said: 'That was *aw*ful. I thought I was going to *die*. I'm ever so sorry.'

'S all right,' said Nicola. 'Not your fault.' She oughtn't to have hesitated: Rose wouldn't have done.

The half hour which followed was decidedly nerve-wracking. They all had to wrap up warm and join their chaperones (mostly other mothers) in something called the Green Room for milk and biscuits while they waited to hear who had been called back to be interviewed by Miss Gover, the Principal, and who was going to be politely told that 'You may go now.'

Most people, including Nicola, drank their milk and nibbled their biscuits in a ghostly kind of silence. Only numbers sixteen and twenty-one, evidently bolder than the rest, continued to jabber and shriek, and even they didn't jabber quite so fiercely or shriek quite so loudly as they had before. The mothers, however, more than made up for it. If they had been at school, thought Nicola, they would all of them have been sent to stand under the clock and collect bad conduct marks a long time ago. She heard Mrs Bruce say:

'Of course, Nicola takes classes from Pamela French. I suppose in a way that gives her an advantage. It means she's already familiar with the Kendra Hall style. But then I don't imagine Mrs French would have taken her on if she hadn't thought she was the right material. She doesn't take just anyone; she's very particular. She doesn't normally accept pupils until they've reached a fairly advanced stage. Of course, she took Nicola when she was only eleven . . . she actually asked me for her.'

Nicola cringed. The only consolation was that all the other mothers were doing it as well.

'Of course, *Lydia's* been learning since she was two years old – '

' – passed *all* her grade exams with distinction – '

' – Fonteyn herself, no less!'

('Stupid woman,' said Mrs Bruce, later. 'As if someone like Fonteyn would lower herself . . . probably doesn't know the child from a hole in the road.')

At the end of thirty minutes Miss Flowerdew came back into the room and smiled and said she would like numbers fourteen, sixteen, nineteen and twenty-one, with their chaperones, to step outside. General apprehension. Did that mean, thank you, you may go – or did it mean, you are being called for an interview?

In the same ghostly silence numbers fourteen, sixteen, nineteen and twenty-one made their way from the room, followed by four grim-faced mothers carrying coats and cardigans and handbags full of glucose tablets and vitamin pills.

'Right, now,' said Miss Flowerdew. 'If you'd care to come this way, Miss Gover would like to speak to you all individually.'

The four mothers exchanged glances of triumph. Number twenty-one, who was bold, gave a big, happy grin; the others just gulped and swallowed and grew a bit pink (or in Nicola's case white: she always turned white when she was anxious).

Miss Gover was the severe-looking elderly lady with gold-rimmed spectacles who had been present at the audition. She was with the little spider man, whom she introduced as Mr Bregonzi. (His name was in the prospectus, at the head of the list of teaching staff. He mainly took the senior boys and advanced *pas de deux*.) To Nicola's relief, Mrs Bruce had been asked if she would mind waiting outside. She didn't like having to talk to people in front of her mother, it made it impossible, sometimes, to say what you really wanted to say. By herself she didn't mind talking to anybody.

Miss Gover asked most of the questions – all about how long she had been doing ballet and what made her think she wanted to be a dancer and was she prepared for all the hard work and dedication involved? To the last question Nicola said yes, she was, because she had had to drop out of the under-fifteen hockey eleven just a few days ago *and* hadn't been able to go swimming or play table tennis because of all the extra classes she was having. Mr Bregonzi said: 'And how do you feel about that? Do you resent it?'

'Sometimes,' said Nicola.

'Do you ever find yourself wishing that you could be just an ordinary schoolgirl? *Not* doing ballet?'

'Mm . . .' She wrinkled her nose, considering. 'I think I *am* quite ordinary, actually, but sometimes I wish that you could do ballet without having to stop doing other things.'

'That,' said Miss Gover, 'would be having you cake and eating it.'

'Yes, I know,' said Nicola.

'And that, as you must realize, is not possible.'

'No,' said Nicola.

96

'So, then – ' Miss Gover removed her spectacles. Her eyes, without them, looked pale and staring, like the eyes of a fish. 'Are there any questions that you would like to ask us? Anything about the school, about the classes?'

Nicola thought for a while; then shyly she said: 'I'd like to know if I could still do physics and chemistry.'

'Physics and chemistry?' Miss Gover turned to look at Mr Bregonzi. 'That's a strange one! We've never had that before.'

Mr Bregonzi leaned forward.

'Why did you want to know?'

'Well, because if I stayed on at school I could do it, and I just thought it would be nice if I could still do it if I came to Kendra Hall – I mean, if I were accepted. But maybe . . . ' (maybe she shouldn't have said anything about it in the first place) ' . . . maybe it's another cake thing, like not being able to play hockey.'

'Yes, I'm afraid it is,' said Miss Gover. 'We simply don't have room on the curriculum to cover the full academic syllabus. I wish we did, but there just aren't enough hours in the day. You'll find you have your work cut out as it is. If, of course – ' she re-settled her spectacles on her nose ' – we are able to offer you a place. I hope that we shall be, but you do realize that we have literally hundreds of applicants every year and only a very few vacancies? Particularly in your age group. Anyway,' she smiled; a rather frost-nipped smile, but still a smile, 'one way or another you'll be hearing from us within a week or two. So until then – '

'Just contain yourself in patience.' Mr Bregonzi also smiled. It was a friendlier smile than Miss Gover's. 'I know that's easier said than done, but . . . do your best!'

After the interview came the medical examination,

with the big plump smiling lady, who laughed a lot and said she thought she could safely promise that Nicola would never grow as big as she was *width*wise, but lengthwise was another matter: by the time she reached her full height she might very possibly be pushing the limit, which for girls was 5' 7".

'Not that there aren't plenty of dancers who are taller than that, so if you do start shooting up there's no need to despair, it's just that they really do like to have Miss Average for the corps de ballet . . . it ruins their pretty patterns if they have one lanky beanpole amidst a neat little forest of garden canes.'

It had always been one of her mother's greatest dreads that Nicola would turn into a lanky beanpole. She fretted at it all the way home.

'It really would be too bad if they turned you down just for that. I still can't think where you get it from . . . *I*'m not tall, your father's not tall . . . tell me again what Miss Gover said to you.'

She had already told her mother what Miss Gover had said to her. Dutifully she repeated it.

'She said she hoped they'd be able to offer me a place but they had hundreds of applicants and I'd be hearing from them in a week or two.'

'What happened before that? What sort of questions did she ask you?'

'Mm . . . she asked me if I minded not being able to play hockey and things.'

'And what did you say?'

'I said sometimes I did, but – '

'You shouldn't have said that!' Mrs Bruce sounded agitated. 'She was obviously trying to find out how much ballet meant to you! What on earth made you go and say a thing like that for?'

'Well, it's true,' said Nicola. 'I *do* sometimes resent it.'

'*Resent?*' Now her mother sounded even more agitated. 'I hope you didn't use that word to Miss Gover?'

'They used it. Then Mr Bregonzi asked me if I ever wished I could be just an ordinary schoolgirl and I said I thought I *was* quite ordinary, but – '

'But what?'

'Well, I just said there were *some* times when I wished you could still do ballet and not have to give up other things. Like yesterday when Cheryl and Sarah came round and you wouldn't let me go out on my bike because you said I'd be sure to do something stupid like falling off and bruising myself and not being fit for the audition . . . . I just wished I could go out on my bike *and* do the audition.'

Her mother looked at her, appalled.

'You didn't tell them that?'

'Yes.' Why shouldn't she have told them? 'They asked me – they wanted to know. They were *interested*. They wouldn't have asked if they weren't, would they?'

Mrs Bruce shook her head.

'Honestly, Nicola,' she said, 'there are times when I simply despair of you.'

8

Contain yourself in patience, Mr Bregonzi had said. Nicola tried her best, but as even Mr Bregonzi had admitted, containing oneself in patience was easier said than done. She went for bicycle rides with Cheryl and Sarah, spent hours drinking milk shakes in the Body Shop, played table tennis and went swimming with Denny, did all the things which she hadn't been able to do before the audition; but every morning she went flying downstairs to look at the post, and every time the telephone rang waited breathlessly, hanging over the banisters or with one ear pressed to a crack in the door, as her mother answered it. (After all, they hadn't said *how* she would hear from them, only that she would do so in a week or two. They might just as easily telephone as write a letter.)

The week or two came and went: the day the summer term began was the day on which she should have heard. As she arrived at school Linda Baker came bustling up.

'Well?' she said, all bossy and dictatorial. 'What happened? Did you get in?'

'Don't know yet,' said Nicola. 'Haven't heard.'

'Haven't *heard*? After all this time?'

'That's a bad sign,' said Janice Martin. 'If they're going to offer you a place they usually do it straight away.'

'They said a week or two,' said Nicola.

'That's what they *say*.'

'When my brother tried for university,' said Sarah, 'he didn't hear for weeks and *weeks*. And then they suddenly wrote and said he'd got in.'

'That's university.' Linda Baker spoke witheringly. 'It's not the same as ballet school.'

Just before assembly, Denny came up to her.

'Didja hear yet?'

She shook her head.

'Probably come in the second post,' said Denny. 'My mum was expecting something this morning and that didn't come, either.'

She was grateful to Denny for trying to cheer her up, but she had a nagging suspicion that Janice Martin might be right: if they had been going to offer her a place they would surely have done so by now? Miss Gover had warned her that they had only a few vacancies, and then there was the possibility that she might grow too tall, and probably she *oughtn't* to have said that bit about sometimes feeling resentful, even if it had been true.

The first period on the starting day of a new term was always devoted to general discussion and the election of class monitors. Sarah put Nicola's name forward for rounders captain, and Miss Camfield looked inquiringly at her.

'Will that be all right, Nicola? I take it you'll be able to play?'

She remembered what Denny had said: like being an *in*valid . . . Linda Baker, who had also been put up for rounders captain, waved a hand.

'She hasn't heard yet whether she's got in or not.'

'No, well, these things take time. In the meantime – ' Miss Camfield turned, and under *Linda Baker* wrote *Nicola Bruce*. 'Anyone else?'

101

One of the boys, who shouldn't have had anything to do with it, since the boys didn't play rounders, said 'Michelle Brown' and everyone jeered, not so much because Michelle Brown was easily the world's worst rounders player but because everyone knew that she and Alan Argent had a thing going. Nicola was glad that she and Denny didn't embarrass each other like that.

Voting took place by a show of hands, with Nicola being elected captain and Linda Baker vice-captain. Linda Baker wasn't terribly pleased because last year it had been the other way round, only lots of people had complained about her bossiness and how rude she was and had threatened to rebel. Sarah, leaning backwards in her chair, whispered: 'Hope you get into ballet school, but I hope you don't have to resign from being captain 'cause if you do I'm not playing under *her* again.'

After all the monitors and team captains had been elected Miss Camfield said they really ought to spend a bit of time discussing future plans, because this was the term when they had to decide which stream they wanted to enter next year: languages, science, or general studies. Denny was going into the science stream: he had known ever since junior school that he wanted to work with computers. Sarah was languages and Cheryl was general studies, which meant that for the first time since juniors the three of them, Sarah, Cheryl and Nicola, were going to be split up. They had talked about it quite often, trying to find a solution, but there just didn't seem to be one. Sarah was hopeless at anything scientific, Cheryl was only good at needlework (she had already made Nicola promise that when she was famous she would let Cheryl design her dresses for her) and no one had any doubts but that Nicola would go on to the science side.

'Let's start at the back,' said Miss Camfield. 'Alan,

what ideas have you got?'

Somebody said, 'Get Michelle Brown behind a bush,' and most of the boys and quite a few of the girls guffawed. (Nicola couldn't see whether Denny did or not. She hoped that he didn't, but as Mrs Bruce always said, tight-lipped, 'Boys are like that.')

Alan Argent was one of those people without a thought in their heads; Nicola didn't know why Miss Camfield wasted her breath trying to communicate with him. Some of the others weren't much better. Some, on the other hand, like Denny and Sarah (who wanted to work in a travel agency so that she could get free flights to places like America and Russia) had lots of thoughts and were only too willing to express them. Nicola would have been willing to express hers if Miss Camfield had asked her – she was quite ready to explain how if she didn't get into ballet school she was going to try for university and study to become a doctor – but disappointingly Miss Camfield didn't bother. All she said when she reached Nicola was, 'Nicola, you're waiting for the result of your audition, of course. Cheryl, how about you?' and they all had to listen to Cheryl rambling on about her needlework.

On the way home that afternoon (across the Common, only now they went by a different route, one which couldn't be seen from the tops of buses) Denny said: 'What're you all jittery for?'

'I'm not all jittery,' said Nicola; but now that he had mentioned it, she knew he was right: she *was* all jittery. She had been jittery all day long.

'Is it because of not hearing?'

'S'pose so.'

Up until now she had just about been able to contain herself. Today, because this was the day when the two weeks were up, she had hardly been able to think of anything else. She had listened while the others babbled and burbled about school affairs, and for the first time it had all seemed so terribly small and unimportant: the only thing that mattered was the result of her audition.

'What'll you do,' said Denny, 'if you don't get in?'

Go away and howl, all by herself. She had already made plans for it. She was going to take Ben and they were going to go off together on a long, long walk, just the two of them, not even Denny, until she was strong enough to face the world again. The last thing she would be able to bear would be to stay indoors and hear Rose commiserating and telling her how Susie Siegenberg's sister hadn't got in either. And her mother alternately grumbling at her for having ruined her chances and bewailing the fact that it was because she was too tall . . . 'I *still* don't know where you get it from.' When Nicola was upset, she liked to be alone.

'Would you try for somewhere else?' said Denny.

'Not sure. Don't think so.'

'Why not? You would if it was university. You wouldn't just try one place and then give up.'

'N-no, but – ' This was different. If she failed Kendra Hall, she didn't really think that she would want to go anywhere else. Maybe the Royal Ballet School, but even that wouldn't be the same. Kendra Hall was where Mrs French had gone, and where she wanted Nicola to go.

'Seems to me,' said Denny, 'you can't want to do it as badly as all that.'

She wanted to get into *Kendra Hall* as badly as all that: she wanted to get into Kendra Hall more than anything else in the world. Denny couldn't understand, there was no point in trying to explain to him. To people who weren't dancers, one ballet school probably seemed very much the same as any other.

'Don't let's talk about it.' Deliberately, trying to make believe she didn't care, she gave a little twirl – and then stopped. Giving little twirls in public places was behaving like Rose. Furthermore, it embarrassed people. She fell back a pace and slipped her hand into Denny's.

'Did you laugh, this morning, when Mark Humphries made that joke?'

'What joke?'

'About Alan Argent wanting to take Michelle Brown behind a bush.'

'Didn't hear it,' said Denny.

'*Would* you have done, if you had?'

'Prob'ly.' Denny grinned. 'Girls like Michelle Brown, not much else you can do with 'em.'

'Don't be *pig*like.' Nicola swung her duffle bag, catching him a hearty biff on the arm. Sometimes she didn't wonder at her mother not liking boys: if even Denny were 'like that' then what hope was there for the rest of them?

The first thing Nicola did on arriving home was say hallo to Ben (it was the first thing that anyone did: there was simply no escaping it). The second thing she did was snatch a quick glance at the kitchen table.

Nothing. Her heart dropped like a chunk of stone, clank-thump, down into her shoes. Whenever there were letters for either Rose or Nicola, Mrs Bruce always put them by the side of their plates, ready for opening. Not that there usually *was* anything for Nicola, except on those occasions when she had written away for catalogues or free samples. There was quite often something for Rose, because children who had seen her on television wrote her fan letters asking for photographs or wanting to know how they could get on television and do the things that she did. Today there was nothing by either of their plates – come to that, there weren't any *plates*. Nicola stared. Where was tea? Where was Mrs Bruce?

'*Hey*!' The door suddenly crashed open and Rose burst in. She grabbed Nicola by the arm. 'I've got something to show you!'

'What?'

'Never mind what!' Rose tugged at her, impatient. 'Come and see!'

'Why?' She wasn't in a mood for being tugged at. She wanted her tea. She wanted bread and jam with lots of butter, and huge squidgy cakes oozing cream that would make her loathsomely and disgustingly fat.

'Just stop asking *questions*,' said Rose.

Disgruntled, Nicola allowed herself to be dragged out of the kitchen, up the hall and into the sitting room.

'*Look*.'

She looked: the table was laid as if for a birthday tea. There were jellies in little cardboard dishes, and bread and butter cut into triangles, and coloured paper napkins, and fruit salad, and a carton of real cream. And right in the middle, a pink-iced cake in the shape of a ballet shoe . . . .

Nicola turned, wonderingly, first to Rose and then to her mother.

'You *see*?' said Rose.

Mrs Bruce was on the telephone, talking excitedly. As Nicola came in, she said: 'Here she is now . . . you can tell her yourself. Nicola!' She flapped a hand. 'Come and talk to your grandmother.'

With one last bewildered glance at the pink-iced cake, Nicola took the receiver that her mother was holding out.

'Gran?'

'Who's a clever girl, then? Now we've got two granddaughters we can boast about! You wait till your grand-dad gets to hear of it. He's down the road at the moment, but the minute he comes back – '

Nicola turned, once again, to look at the table and its array of goodies. She saw now, what she hadn't seen before: by the side of one of the plates there was an envelope. Mrs Bruce picked it up and waved it at her, nodding triumphantly as she did so.

Gran's voice was still speaking at her out of the telephone.

'So how do you feel? Do you feel excited? I do – and I know your mother does! Anyway, my dear, I'll leave you to go and eat your tea, because I'm sure you're having something special, and I expect your grandfather will ring you later. How about that?'

'Yes,' said Nicola. She felt in a daze. She felt as if she were living in *Alice in Wonderland*, and it was all going to turn into a dream. Numbly, she replaced the receiver.

'Here you are!' Mrs Bruce held out the envelope. 'It's yours – take it!'

Nicola did so. She held it a moment, examining it and turning it over in her hands, studying the stamp and the post mark. The envelope had already been opened; untidily ripped, which was the way that Mrs Bruce always opened letters. Nicola, perhaps because she had so few, liked to do the job neatly and carefully, taking her time, slitting the top with a paper-knife or ruler so that when she had removed the letter and read it she could fold it back up and put it away again.

'Aren't you going to look?' shrilled Rose.

Dutifully she removed the sheet of paper from the ruined envelope. (It was addressed to her; quite plainly, on the front in typed letters: *Ms Nicola Bruce, 10 Fenning Road, Streatham, London S.W.16.*) Rose and her mother were watching her, with a kind of eager anticipation.

'Well?' said Mrs Bruce.

Reluctantly Nicola opened the letter out. It wasn't the same, reading a letter that had already been read by someone else.

Dear Nicola,

We are pleased to tell you that we are able to offer you a place at Kendra Hall starting in September of this year.

We hope that you will be able to accept it and that we shall see you here next term.

We shall be writing to your parents in a day or two with details.

Yours sincerely,

Barbara Flowerdew

(Head of Ballet Studies, Junior School)

'*Well?*' Rose was almost dancing on the spot. 'Aren't you going to say anything?'

'It came by the second post,' said Mrs Bruce. 'I thought I'd better open it, just in case it was bad news.'

'Honestly,' said Rose, 'hardly *any*body gets into Kendra Hall. Susie Siegenberg's going to be absolutely *green*.'

'I'd already made the cake,' said Mrs Bruce, 'some time ago. If you hadn't got in, I was going to keep it for your birthday.'

'Look,' said Rose, 'it's even got *ribbons*.'

Sure enough, there were two beautiful pink satin ribbons attached, just where the ribbons on a real ballet shoe would be. They trailed artistically across the table, threading amongst the jellies and little plates of bread and butter.

'I'd have sent you a telegram,' said Rose, 'if there'd been time.'

'Gran and Granpa up north will send a telegram. I rang them immediately, they're as pleased as can be. They said to give you their congratulations. Oh, and I told Mrs French, I knew you'd want her to know. She's over the moon. She said she'll see you tomorrow when you've had time to get over the excitement. There's no point in having a class this evening, you'd never be able to concentrate. We both agreed that a bit of a celebration's in order.'

'Wait till you tell Janice Martin,' said Rose. Rose knew all about Janice Martin, having been at Madam Paula's with her. 'I bet she'll be even greener that Susie Siegenberg.'

'I told Mrs Kemp, up the road. She said she could hardly believe it . . . Nicola's always been such a *gawky* child.' Mrs Bruce laughed, happily. 'I said we hadn't been able to believe it, just at first. I still remember that day Mrs French asked me if you could go and take lessons with her . . . *Nicola?* I said. How could anyone want *Nicola?* Well, she's proved us all wrong!'

'*I* knew,' said Rose. 'That time I let her stand in for me in the mime show.'

Rose hadn't let her stand in for her. Mr Marlowe, who had been the producer, had wanted Nicola in Rose's place, and Rose had sulked and screamed for a week until Nicola had stood down again. She knelt, and put her arms round Ben's neck.

'Aren't you thrilled?' said Rose.

'Course I am.'

'You're not *sounding* it . . . I'd be turning cartwheels!'

'Go and wash your hands,' said Mrs Bruce. 'Let's have some tea.'

Nicola rubbed her cheek against Ben's.

'What did Dad say?'

'Oh, I haven't told your father! You know what he's

like . . . no interest in anything outside his football and his gardening. You can tell him when he comes in.'

She wished she could have told Mrs French. She could still tell Denny, of course, and Cheryl and Sarah – *and* Janice Martin: she would enjoy telling Janice Martin – but Mrs French was the one she had really been looking forward to telling. She had even gone so far, once or twice, as to allow herself the luxury of imagining how it would be . . . running up the road, banging with the big lion's head knocker on Mrs French's front door, Mrs French coming to open it . . . .

Now Mrs French had already been told.

'I wish you'd go and *wash*,' said Rose. 'We can't start eating till you're ready.'

Slowly, Nicola got to her feet.

'Shouldn't we wait till Dad gets in?'

'I'm not waiting till then! I'm *starving*!'

'We'll save him a piece of cake,' said Mrs Bruce. 'You go and scrub those dirty hands while I put the kettle on.'

Obediently Nicola went across to the door.

'What did Mrs French say when you told her?'

'She said, that's absolutely wonderful, I always knew Nicola had it in her – which she did, of course. One has to hand it to her. The rest of us didn't see it, but she did.'

'*I* did,' said Rose.

Rose was such a liar. Nobody had seen it, except for Mrs French. Nicola closed the door behind her and trailed up the stairs, Ben lolloping at her side. Once in the bathroom she turned both taps full on, so that the water swirled and rushed about the bowl, spraying drops all over. Ben, excited, stood and barked.

She didn't care if the carpet did get wet. It was stupid, having a carpet in a bathroom.

111

She didn't care if the neighbours did complain about Ben barking. Dogs ought to be allowed to bark. It was their way of expressing themselves.

She plunged both hands into the gushing water, creating tidal waves. Slop slurp, on to the floor.

'When will you ever learn, Nicola? That carpet will rot if you keep getting it wet.'

That had been *her* letter, addressed to *her*.

People oughtn't to open other people's letters. They hadn't any right.

'I thought I'd better, just in case it was bad news ...'

But it hadn't been bad news. It had been glorious, marvellous, incredibly fantastic news, and this ought to be the most glorious, marvellous, incredibly fantastic moment of her whole life.

She wondered why it was that she suddenly felt like *crying*.

9

'Nicola Tulip – '
  'Nicola *Rose*.'
  Giggle giggle. Great hilarity.
  'Nicola Daffodil – '
  'Nicola Geranium – '
  'Nicola Mi*mos*a!'
  Tee hee. Ho ho. Ha ha.
  'I've told you,' said Nicola. 'I'm staying as I am.'
  She might just as well not have bothered: nobody took
the slightest bit of notice. Cheryl, scrambling on to her
desk lid, raised an imaginary trumpet to her lips.
  'Ta ra ta ra! Introducing, in the far corner . . . Nicola
– Mimosa!'
  'Nicolette de la Mimose – '
  'De la Bruce – '
  'Bruce*los*is!'
  'That's a disease,' said Nicola. 'It's what cows get.'
  Janice Martin sniggered; whether at the display of
ignorance or because she thought it funny that Nicola
might call herself after a disease there was no means of
knowing. Mr Kenny came into the room at that point to
take a geography lesson and all conversation had to
cease. (It didn't stop Janice Martin passing her a note
which read *How about Nicola Bindweed?* Extraordinarily
childish sense of humour some people had.)
  'Would you really want to be famous?' Denny said to

her later, as they walked home. She thought about it.

'Wouldn't mind.'

'I wouldn't,' said Denny.

'*Wouldn't* you?'

He shook his head, very definite.

'I wouldn't mind inventing something and being talked about in magazines and things, but I wouldn't want to be famous like a TV star and have everyone keep on recognizing me all the time.'

'Mm . . . I s'pose it might get a bit of a nuisance.'

'Dead boring,' said Denny.

'But it would be nice to think that everyone had heard of you.'

'Don't see why.'

Upon reflection, Nicola wasn't sure that she could see why, either. After all, what difference would it make?

'You'd get letters,' she said hopefully. 'That'd be nice . . . hundreds and hundreds each day. I'd like that.'

'Bet you wouldn't if you had to answer 'em all.'

'I'd have a secretary; she'd do all the answering. I'd only have to read them.'

Denny grunted, plainly not convinced. Nicola thought about it a bit more.

'P'raps I wouldn't actually want to be *world* famous . . . just a *little* bit famous, so's I'd have just a *few* letters, and just *some*times people'd stop me in the street and say things to me.'

On that basis, though, she already was 'just a little bit famous'. No fewer than three people from Fenning Road had stopped her on the way to school that morning to congratulate her. First there had been Mrs Hope, the lady next door, who had been putting out her milk bottles just as Nicola was leaving; then there had been Mr Kemp, who was the husband of Mrs Kemp, who had 'hardly been able to believe it' (*Nicola was always such a GAWKY child* . . .). Mr Kemp had been getting into his car and had got out of it again to say, 'Splendid piece of news! Well done!' The third person had been crotchety Miss Dunk from number fifteen, whom Rose always referred to as 'the old bag across the road'. Practically the only times Miss Dunk had ever spoken to Nicola were to tell her off for letting Ben cock his leg against her fence or for rattling sticks against the palings or kicking tin cans in the gutter. This morning she had crooked a finger, and when Nicola, reluctantly, had crossed over (*what had she done wrong now?*) beamed at her and said, 'Well! I understand we have a little Anna Pavlova in our midst?' It was rather a yukkish sort of thing to say, but at least it was better than being lectured for bad manners or for noisiness.

'S'pose you reckon you're quite famous already,' said Denny.

She felt her cheeks grow hot.

'Course I don't!'

'Way everyone was carrying on before school this morning, anyone'd think you'd been made Queen of England.'

'Well, that's not my fault!'

Denny said 'Humph!' and hunched a shoulder. She looked at him, crossly. This was just like that other time, when she'd first told him about the audition and he'd behaved so horribly. 'Why are you being so mean?' she said.

Denny kicked a stone.

'I'm not being mean.'

'You are! You're being beastly!'

If it had been Linda Baker or Janice Martin she would have put it down to common-or-garden jealousy, but Denny wasn't like that. He hadn't been jealous when she'd won the second year prize for Hard Work and Endeavour, any more than she'd been jealous when he'd come top in the under-fourteen section of the Computer Club competition organized by the Junior Library. He certainly wouldn't be jealous of her getting into ballet school. She couldn't understand what was making him so grumpy – he hadn't even bothered to congratulate her properly. She'd waited to tell him the news before any of the others and all he'd said was, 'Oh. That's good.'

'I thought you'd be *pleased* for me,' she said.

'I am pleased for you.'

'Then why are you being so horrible?'

This time, he didn't deny that he was being horrible. Keeping his eyes fixed firmly on the ground, he muttered: 'Thought we were going to go into 4S together.'

4S was Class 4, Sciences. Nicola, too, had thought they would be going into it together. She had never seriously dreamed that Mrs French would suggest she try for ballet school – she had never seriously dreamed that having tried for it she would actually be offered a place. Even now she had to shake herself in order to believe it. The fact that this time next term Denny would be in 4S all by himself and she would be at Kendra Hall still hadn't properly sunk in.

'Won't be the same,' said Denny.

'No – ' For the first time, she realized it: everything from now on was going to be quite different. Rose always said that that was what was so wonderful about being in the theatre.

'It's all so *different*. You never have time to get bored . . . I'd rather *die* than have to be in the same place seeing the same people every day.'

Nicola wasn't like Rose; she preferred a certain sameness in life. She actually liked seeing familiar faces all about her and having the comfort of a set routine. Rose, at the age of eleven, had left St Mary's Juniors and gone off to Ida Johnson without so much as a backward glance. When Nicola, a year earlier, had moved up from junior school to senior she had not only gone round every single member of staff begging for autographs but had even kept all her old exercise books and reports, locked away in a big black deed box with the words CHAS. FAULKENDER DEC'D written on it in white lettering which had been given to her by the man who lived next door. Over CHAS. FAULKENDER DEC'D she had stuck a label saying *Nicola Bruce, 10 Fenning Road, Streatham, London, England, Great Britain, The World, Private Papers*, NOT TO BE OPENED UNTIL THE YEAR 2000. Rose said she was completely raving potty. She sighed.

'Won't be able to go over the Common any more,' said Denny.

'No . . . I s'pose not.'

'Won't be able to sit together in Assembly.'

Nicola brightened.

'We'll still be able to go to football matches.'

'Yeah, but it won't be the same,' said Denny. 'Never is.'

When Nicola arrived home there were two letters waiting by the side of her plate; this time, Mrs Bruce had not opened them.

'One's from Auntie Becky,' she said. 'I don't know who the other's from, it's local.'

Auntie Becky had sent a card with a scene from *Coppélia* on the front of it. Inside it said 'Congratulations! All our love, Auntie Becky, Uncle Andrew, Lorna, Doug and Lucy. XXX.'

'Isn't that nice?' said Mrs Bruce. 'All the way from Scotland . . . Gran-up-north must have rung them.'

117

In the other envelope was a card with a funny picture of a mouse drinking from a glass of champagne. Nicola couldn't think who had sent it until she looked inside and saw, 'Good old Supermouse! I always knew you could do it. Love and kisses from your friendly neighbourhood photographer.'

Her mother said: 'Oh, that must be Mr French!'

'It's not Mr French,' said Nicola, 'it's Mr Marlowe.'

'Mr Marlowe? Who's Mr Marlowe?'

Didn't her mother remember *any*thing?

'He's the one that produced the mime show . . . that time they wanted me instead of Rose.'

Her mother glanced nervously towards the kitchen door. (Nicola guessed that Rose must be somewhere out there.)

'Why should he be sending you a card?'

Why shouldn't he? She and Mr Marlowe had been friends.

'He used to call me Supermouse.'

'So what's this bit about your friendly neighbourhood photographer?'

'That's a joke,' said Nicola. 'Cause he played a photographer in the mime show.'

'Hm.' Mrs Bruce seemed doubtful; as if secretly, inside herself, she was still convinced that it was Mr French. She swept the cards up and put them on top of the kitchen cabinet. 'You'll have to start a scrapbook. Remind me tomorrow, I'll go and buy you one. Incidentally – ' she opened the refrigerator, pushing Ben's head out of the way as she did so (Ben's head having a tendency to get into refrigerators and help itself). 'Mrs Kemp asked me, as you won't be going back to St Mary's next term, whether she could have your blazer for Alison.'

'What for?' She resented her blazer being given away,

118

especially to someone like Alison Kemp, who had once gone screaming home to her mother complaining that 'Nicola Bruce made her dog go for me.' She hadn't made Ben go for her, you couldn't make Ben go for anyone, probably not even burglars, he was far too sloppy. All he'd done was jump up to say hallo and accidentally knock her over. 'What's she want my blazer for?'

'It would come in very handy,' said Mrs Bruce. 'Assuming, of course, there's any wear left in it.'

'I don't expect there will be.' There jolly well *wouldn't* be, if she had anything to do with it. The thought of Alison Kemp inside her blazer made her feel quite sick.

'It shouldn't be in too bad a state,' said Mrs Bruce. 'Especially if it's a hot summer and you don't wear it all that much.'

She would wear it and wear it as hard as she could go. She would wear it even if it gave her heat strokes – even if it sweated her nigh unto *death*.

'Anyway, I told Mrs Kemp she'd be welcome to it, so if you could just refrain from doing anything silly – '

What could she do that was silly?

'I could accidentally set fire to it,' she said, 'with a box of matches.'

Mrs Bruce placed the milk jug on the table and pushed Ben's paws back where they belonged, on the floor.

'Really, Nicola,' she said, 'I don't know why you're being such a dog in the manger. *You'll* be at Kendra Hall . . . *you* won't need the blazer any more.'

On Friday in biology, Miss Richardson said they were going to dissect a mouse.

'It's a mouse that Toby brought in, so I thought we'd take the opportunity to open it up.'

Toby was Miss Richardson's cat and quite often brought

her presents of small creatures that he had slaughtered. Miss Richardson didn't believe in wantonly killing animals just so that people could dissect them, she preferred to use slides, and organs already pickled in formalin, but as she said, you couldn't stop a cat following the course of nature. It was sad when Toby killed fledglings and tiny little creeping things that did no one any harm, but once he had done so it seemed silly not to make use of them.

Everyone gathered round to watch as Miss Richardson, in her white lab. coat, neatly made the first incision. Sarah, who was genuinely squeamish, and Janice Martin, who liked to pretend to be so because she thought it showed how sensitive she was, both turned away.

'Poor little thing,' said Miss Richardson. 'It was pregnant . . . look.'

Nicola craned forward to see. She would never have killed a mouse herself, any more than Miss Richardson would. She had once had a mouse of her own, a white one with brown ears, called Humphrey. Rose had been terrified and yelled every time she saw him, so that in the end Mrs Bruce had set him loose in the garden where almost certainly he would have fallen prey to a marauding monster like Toby. Nicola couldn't have watched Humphrey being dissected to save her life, but this was a mouse quite unknown to her.

'What's that?' She pointed. 'Is that the liver?'

'That's right. Do you want to try taking it out?'

Nicola held out her hand eagerly for the dissecting knife. Cheryl said, '*Ugh*.' Linda Baker made a vomiting noise.

'Just think,' said Miss Richardson, pleasantly, 'this is what we all look like inside.'

Someone said: 'Imagine being a *surgeon* . . . having to cut people up.'

Linda Baker pretended to vomit again. Cheryl said: 'I couldn't.'

'I could,' said Nicola. She thought it would be fascinating, poking around inside people's bodies, taking out those bits that weren't any good any more, patching up other bits that had got broken or gone wrong. She wondered if she would rather be a surgeon than an ordinary doctor, just listening to heart beats and handing out medicines. Surgery would probably be more exciting. Perhaps she might even perfect some marvellous technique for transplanting organs that had never been transplanted before, such as stomachs or windpipes or something. Stomachs sounded as if they might be possible. She looked down at the mouse, working out how it could be done.

'Can I take its stomach out, as well?'

'Yes, all right,' said Miss Richardson. 'Unless there's anyone else who'd like to try?'

Silence. (Apart from another pretend vomit from Linda Baker and another shudder from Cheryl.)

'Off you go then,' said Miss Richardson. 'Be very careful.'

It was strange, but when Nicola was given a needle and cotton and told to sew a hem she instantly became all fingers and thumbs: her stitches, huge and all too visible, galloped wildly in switchback fashion, and almost always the material ended up splotched with blood, so that now Mrs Hibbert insisted she choose only dark colours so the blood wouldn't show. When it came to dissecting a mouse, which was a far more fiddly task, owing to a mouse being so incredibly tiny, her fingers behaved themselves perfectly without any of their usual clumsiness and stupidity.

'Excellent!' said Miss Richardson. 'What a nice neat job! You really seem to have a feel for it. Have you ever

actually thought of becoming a surgeon, Nicola?'

There was a moment's pause. Nicola waited for some loud-mouth, such as Linda Baker, to say, 'She's going to be a dancer,' but nobody did. They were probably all waiting for her to say it herself. Awkwardly she said: 'I did think once that I might quite like to be a doctor.'

'Well, try thinking about being a surgeon. We could do with a few more women in that field . . . it's still very much a male preserve.' Miss Richardson nodded as she took back her dissecting knife. 'Remind me to have a serious talk with you about it next term; discuss the possibilities. It might well be something you could work towards.'

Again, Nicola waited for someone to say 'She won't be here next term.' Again, nobody did. The class continued, but somehow, for Nicola, the joy had gone out of it.

'Why didn't you *tell* her?' hissed Cheryl, as they filed out at the end.

'I thought she'd know.' In her terrible conceit, she had thought that everyone would know; everyone from Mr Henry down to the lowliest and most insignificant of first years. She blushed now to think of it. There were eight hundred pupils in the school; who should know or care what one totally unimportant third year was doing?

'You should have told her,' said Cheryl. 'She thinks you're going to be a surgeon now.'

'She'll wonder where you are when you don't come back next term,' said Sarah.

'Why didn't you *say* something'

'You should have said *some*thing.'

'Well, I didn't,' snapped Nicola, 'so you can just shut up!

She raced off down the corridor, bumping people with

her bag, heedless of the angry cries from the prefect on corridor duty: 'No running! I said, *no running* . . . you there! Come back!'

Nicola wasn't as a rule disobedient; not unless there was a reason for it. Today there wasn't any reason – or none that she could see. All she knew was that for the second time in a week she felt like crying, which was ridiculous. It simply made no sense.

She had got what she wanted, she had got a place at ballet school. What on earth was there to cry about?

10

Every year in June St Mary's had a Parents' Week, when the school was kept open in the evenings for parents to come in and talk to teachers and look round the classrooms. In the past Mrs Bruce had never bothered with Parents' Week; she had always said that she knew what progress Nicola was making from reading her reports, so why should she need to come and talk to teachers?

'They'll tell us quickly enough if she's not behaving herself.'

This year, for the first time, she decided that it was her duty to attend. When Nicola asked her 'What for?' she said, 'Because it's your last term there,' which seemed a strange reason to Nicola. You would have thought since it *was* her last term, there would be less reason than ever, but once Mrs Bruce had made up her mind she stood firm: she was going, and that was that. Nicola was also going, and so was Mr Bruce. Nicola said, 'Why *me*? Why have I got to come?' Mr Bruce, surprisingly, said, 'Yes, all right. That's probably a good idea.'

For her part Nicola thought it was a rotten, lousy idea. She wouldn't have minded if they had gone *last* June – in fact she would quite have liked them to go last June. Denny's parents always went, and so did Cheryl's and Sarah's. She had often wondered why it was that neither of hers ever bothered, especially when she had done well and got a prize essay pinned on the wall or had her name included in the Highly Commended list on the Sports Notice Board. They had never seen any of that, and now when it was too late (because what was the point when she wasn't going to be there any more?) they had to decide to go, and to drag her along with them.

'What about my class?' she said. 'I'm supposed to be having a class tonight.'

'I've spoken to Mrs French, you don't need to worry about that. She says it won't hurt you to miss class just for once. In fact I think she was secretly quite glad. She's very near her time, she'll be having the baby in a week or two; she could do with a bit of a break.'

'How long does it take to have a baby?' said Nicola.

'What do you mean, how long does it take? It takes nine months! I thought you were the one that was supposed to be so hot on biology?'

'No, I mean, actually *having* it.'

'Oh! Well, that depends. It could take an hour or so – it could take all day and all night. When I had you it happened so fast I hardly knew anything about it. Rose, on the other hand, was an absolute little monster . . . took for ever.'

It was good to know that for once it had been Rose and not herself causing trouble, but that hadn't really been why she had asked.

'How long do you have to stay in hospital?'

'Not very long. A few days, perhaps.'

'And then you can just carry on the same as normal?'

'More or less, yes.'

'So how many lessons will Mrs French be away for?'

'Oh, I should think she'd probably give herself at least a fortnight, if not a month. But I'm sure she'll arrange for you to have classes with someone else.'

'Oh.' She hadn't thought of that. She had told Denny that while Mrs French was away she wouldn't be having classes and could go swimming and play table tennis as much as he liked. 'I don't think I'd want to have classes with someone else.'

'It's not a question of what you want, it's a question of what Mrs French decides is best for you. Anyway, it'll help you get accustomed to the idea – after all, you won't be having Mrs French when you're at Kendra Hall. Where has that man got to?' Mrs Bruce looked in exasperation at her watch. 'It's time we were off. Why does he always have to go and disappear at the last minute?'

'He went into the garden,' said Nicola. 'I'll get him.' She found Mr Bruce tucked away between two rows of runner beans. 'It's time to go,' she said.

'Is it? All right. Tell your mother I'm just coming.'

Obediently she went back indoors and delivered the message. Mrs Bruce clicked her tongue crossly against the roof of her mouth.

'Men!' she said.

There were times when Nicola really wondered why her mother had ever got married. She was sure *she* never would, if she hated men as much as all that. Luckily she didn't so probably one day she would, though just at the moment it was hard to envisage it, because how could you be sure you wouldn't quarrel and fight? Even with Denny she had differences of opinion, which sometimes developed into full-scale arguments, but perhaps you couldn't ever hope to meet anyone you agreed with absolutely and totally all of the time; not if you were the sort of person who *thought*. Miss Richardson said it was very important to be a person who thought.

Her father appeared, wiping earth off his hands with

his handkerchief (more angry tongue-clicking from Mrs Bruce) and they set off up the road towards the school.

'Where d'you want to go first?' said Nicola.

'Well, I suppose we'd better go and see your class teacher, hadn't we? Miss Cameron, or whatever her name is.'

'Camfield,' said Nicola.

Mr Bruce, who had been lingering in the main entrance hall studying the photographs of the school football and hockey elevens, called out: 'Isn't she the one that said you were an asset to the community?'

'Yes.' Nicola cast an agonized glance over her shoulder: fortunately no one was within hearing distance. It was nice that her father should have remembered the comment, but she wished he wouldn't shout about it.

'Go on, then!' Mrs Bruce gave her a little push. 'Lead the way.'

3B's classroom was empty apart from Linda Baker and her mother, who were talking to Miss Camfield, and a couple of parents whom Nicola didn't recognize but who had presumably already done their talking because they were on their way out. Miss Camfield glanced up and smiled as she saw Nicola. She'll wonder why we've come, thought Nicola. After all, there wasn't any *point* in coming; not now.

'What's all this stuff on the walls?' Mr Bruce wanted to know.

'Just bits of work that people have done that have got good marks.'

'Have you got anything up there?'

'Bit of biology.'

'Well, let's see it, then!'

She led them across to her drawing of the inside of a rabbit, with all the organs done in different colours and